DOOM PLATOON

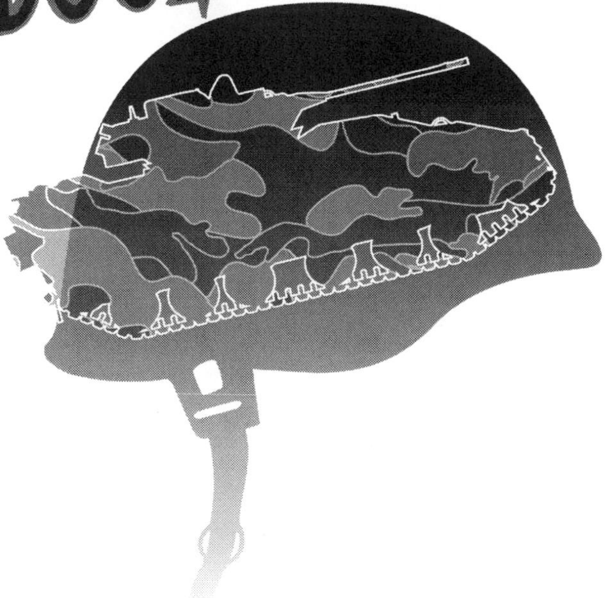

Len Levinson
(writing as Richard Gallagher)

DOOM PLATOON
By Len Levinson writing as Leonard Jordan
First published by Belmont Tower in 1978

Cover image © 2015 by Destroyer Books
Print edition cover designed by Alyssa Brewer
E-book edition cover designed by Ayla Elliott
Published by arrangement with the author.

For more information on this title, or any of our other titles, please contact the publisher at destroyerbooks@gmail.com.

ISBN-10: 1-944073-00-0
ISBN-13: 978-1-944073-00-8

Chapter One

THE SHELL ROARED OVERHEAD and exploded a few hundred yards away.

Sergeant Mazursky opened his eyes. "What the fuck was that?"

"An artillery shell," replied Corporal Dooley, who had been sleeping next to Mazursky in the pup tent.

"I know it was a fucking artillery shell."

"Then why'd you ask?"

Mazursky grunted something unintelligible.

"Go back to sleep," said Dooley. "Some German must've leaned on his cannon by mistake, and it went off."

Mazursky sat up and put on his steel helmet. He was 32 years old, unshaven, and looked mean. He didn't think the German cannon went off by mistake. Reaching into the breast pocket of his field jacket, he took out a half-smoked cigar, putting it in his mouth. He lit it with his trusty old Zippo. In the light of the Zippo he looked at his watch. It was 0530 hours in the morning of December 16, 1944, and his regiment was on the front line in the Ardennes Forest of France.

There was another shell explosion, this one a few hundred yards to the front.

Dooley sat up and reached for his helmet. "Oh shit," he murmured.

"Artillery attack," said Mazursky. "We'd better get into the trench."

"Oh fuck."

They strung bandoliers of ammunition around their shoulders and clipped hand grenades to their lapels. Then they dragged their M-1 rifles out of the pup tent. It was a cold, wintry night and there was a thin layer of ice on top of the snow. Their breath made clouds of smoke as they struck the tent, unbuttoned it, and pulled each half with their packs toward the trench. Looking up into the sky, they could see no moon or stars. That meant no air cover, because the Air Corps didn't fly in weather like this. Before they reached the trench a shell landed within their company area, and they dropped to their stomachs on the snow. The explosion knocked over a few tall trees, and sent dirt and snow flying through the air. They leapt up, ran to the trench, and dove in.

"They've got our range," said Dooley, his back against the wall of the trench. He was tall and slim, with red hair and a lantern jaw.

"I think they knew pretty much where we were."

"I wonder what's going on?"

"How the fuck should I know?"

Five more shells landed nearly simultaneously in the company area. Mazursky sat on his haunches and puffed his cigar. He'd fought in Sicily and he'd been in the first wave that went ashore on Normandy Beach. A professional soldier, he'd joined the Army in 1935 when he was twenty years old. This was the third time he'd been a sergeant; he'd been busted the two other times because he had a tendency to get drunk and disorderly while on pass.

The trench began to fill up with members of the Second Platoon, leaping and diving into the trench from all directions, dragging pup tents, packs, rifles, and C-rations.

Private Morelli of Brooklyn landed beside Mazursky and looked at him. "I thought this was supposed to be a fucking rest area."

"So did I," muttered Mazursky, chewing his cigar.

The 25th Regiment had been sent to the Ardennes after taking a terrible mauling in the Hurtgen Forest campaign only three days before. They'd suffered heavy casualties, and now were under strength and battle-fatigued. The Ardennes Forest was considered the safest part of the Allied front line, because the trees and hills made maneuverability difficult for the motorized armies of the Third Reich. The Germans would never attack here, it was thought, and besides, the Germans were being thrown back everywhere. It was unlikely that they'd ever be able to mount a major attack again.

But in the forward salient of the Ardennes line, shells rained down on Charlie Company. They didn't know it, but it was the beginning of the Battle of the Bulge.

"Sergeant Mazursky!" called out the familiar voice of Lieutenant Smith.

"Over here!" yelled Mazursky.

Lieutenant Smith came crawling through the trench,

the silver bar of his rank in the center of his helmet. His eyes burned like two hot coals, his cheeks had been hollowed out by six months of front-line warfare, and he had a tendency to chew his lips whenever he was nervous, which was almost always. He was followed by Pfc. Sheldon Stein, his runner. Stein carried a walkie-talkie, a bazooka, and an M-1 carbine.

"Looks like we're going to get attacked," Smith said to Mazursky.

"Looks that way."

"I think you'd better tell the men to fix bayonets."

"FIX BAYONETS!" Mazursky screamed.

There was rustling and clanking in the trench as the men unhooked their bayonets and fastened them to the barrels of their rifles. Mazursky looked at Smith. Artillery shells were making their ears ring, and the earth trembled beneath their feet.

"If we get attacked, we're going to be in trouble," Mazursky said. "We don't have much people, and we're stretched awfully thin."

"Maybe they won't have much people either."

"They wouldn't be throwing all this artillery at us if they didn't mean to back it up with troops."

"I don't think their main attack will come here. They can't drive tanks through these woods."

"The road to Dillendorf is less than a two miles away. They might want to secure these woods so they can use that road. And you know what's in Dillendorf."

"Oil."

"Right."

4

Smith took off his helmet and ran his fingers through his blond hair. He thought of his wife in Des Moines and wondered what she was doing right now. A shell came whistling down and they all fell in the bottom of the trench. The shell landed about twenty yards away, filling the air with smoke and phosphorous. Smith raised himself on his knees and chewed his lips.

"I think we should get the hell out of here," Smith said.

"That's okay by me," Mazursky replied.

"I already called the CO. He said he'd reported our situation and was awaiting orders himself."

"They're probably fucking around, putting pins in maps at Division. Meanwhile we're liable to get overrun."

"They'll have to overrun Company A and B first. They'll tip us off."

"Yeah," said Mazursky, but he wasn't so sure. He didn't believe anything unless he saw it with his own eyes, or heard it with his own ears.

Pfc. Stein had his ear pressed to the walkie-talkie. He spoke a few words into it, then tapped Smith on the shoulder. "Shanahan wants to speak to you, Lieutenant." Shanahan was the company executive officer.

Lieutenant Smith took the walkie-talkie, held it to his ear, and pressed the button. "Smith here."

"What's going on up there?"

"Heavy bombardment. Can't you hear it?"

"See anything?"

"Just the inside of this trench."

"You don't have lookouts posted?"

"Yeah. There's nothing but shells exploding. When the shells stop coming in, that's when we have to worry."

"The Old Man wants to see you. Get here as soon as you can."

"What do you hear from Division?"

"I said get here as soon as you can. That's an order. Over and out."

Smith handed the walkie-talkie back to Stein and looked at Mazursky. "That was Shanahan. The Old Man wants to see me. Take charge of the platoon."

"Yes sir."

"You'd better stick your head up every once in a while to see what's going on out there."

"Yes sir."

"If the shelling stops, prepare for an attack."

"Yes sir."

Lieutenant Smith looked at Pfc. Stein. "Let's go to see the Old Man."

"Yes sir."

Smith and Stein went up over the side of the trench and crawled over the snow and dirt toward company headquarters, a bunker around 75 yards back. Mazursky watched them go, but then a shell came whistling down and he hit the dirt. He cursed himself for not asking Lieutenant Smith to ask the Old Man for permission to pull back, or for reinforcements. If neither of those two things happened, the situation might get a little serious in the second platoon.

"Who's got the other fucking walkie-talkie!" he yelled.

"I do," replied a voice down the trench, a voice he recognized as belong to Pfc. Albright.

"Bring it over here."

Albright, a chubby 18-year-old from Toledo, squeezed his way down the trench with the walkie-talkie.

Mazursky took it from him, pressed the button, and spoke the call letters of the fourth platoon, which was the heavy weapons platoon.

He was answered by the platoon sergeant, whose name was Rawls.

"I was wondering," Mazursky said, "how you've got your mortars set up."

"Do I call you and ask how you've got your clowns set up?"

"You should have them zeroed in on an area extending from about fifty yards in front of our position up to the point of your farthest visibility. Do you have them that way?"

"No."

"Why not?"

"Hey Mazursky, this isn't your platoon anymore, remember? This is my platoon."

"How do you have them set up?"

"They're aimed on the other side of Hill 103."

"What the fuck good is that supposed to do?"

"Them's my orders."

"When did you get those orders?"

"When we got here three days ago."

"But we're under attack right now."

"I still ain't had no new orders yet."

"You're in charge of the platoon now. You give the orders."

"I ain't doing nothing until Lieutenant Ledoux tells me."

Mazursky chewed his cigar. Ledoux must have gone to the meeting with the Old Man "What are your machine guns doing?"

"Don't worry about my machine guns."

"You've got to have overlapping fields of fire, Rawls. There can't be any holes. We're liable to get attacked any minute."

"I don't have time for this conversation, Mazursky."

"You'd better change those mortars around. It don't make sense to have them aimed where you're aiming them."

"When you become the company commander, then you can start telling me where to put my mortars. Until then, over and out."

Mazursky chewed his cigar and handed the walkie-talkie back to Pfc. Albright. "Fucking asshole," he muttered.

"Who me?" asked Albright.

"No, Rawls, But you're an asshole too."

"What'd l do?"

"Shut up and don't go too far away with that walkie-talkie."

Mazursky relit the stub of his cigar. Something told him that the attack would be coming pretty soon. He hoped orders to pull back would come before the attack, but he couldn't rely on headquarters to save his ass. He'd have to try to save it himself. A shell exploded at the rim of the trench, splattering him with mud. He wiped it off his face and went drawling down the trench, positioning his men, telling them to get ready to shoot fast and throw lots of hand grenades. He was especially careful with his BAR men, because they had the only automatic weapons in the platoon.

One of the BAR men, Private Nowicki of Pittsburgh,

had his BAR taken apart on his poncho at the bottom of the trench.

Mazursky crawled up to him. "What in the dogshit do you think you're doing?"

"I'm cleaning my BAR."

"Now?"

"Yes sergeant."

"You should've cleaned it last night."

"I did clean it last night."

"Then what're you cleaning it now for?"

"Because I wanna make sure it doesn't jam."

"I think your fucking head is jammed. Don't you know we're gonna be attacked any minute?"

"That's why I wanna make sure my BAR is working right."

Mazursky glared at him. "You fucking dimwit, you'd better put that weapon together right now or I'll kick your head in."

"Yes sergeant."

Corporal Ginsberg, leader of the first squad, came crawling over. "What's the problem here, sergeant?"

Mazursky took his cigar out of his mouth and held it in the tips of his fingers. "Your man is taking his BAR apart and we might be attacked at any moment."

"He was just making sure it wasn't jammed, sergeant."

Mazursky looked at Nowicki. "Why don't you fire it to make sure it isn't jammed?"

Nowicki shrugged his massive shoulders. "Because it might get jammed after I fire it. The only way to tell for sure is to examine those little holes in the compression chamber."

"I think you've got little holes in your head, Nowicki.

No, I take that back. I think you got big holes in your head." Mazursky turned to Ginsberg. "Why do you let this idiot take his BAR apart at times like this?"

Ginsberg sniffed and wiped his nose with the back of his hand. "Because he gets very nervous if I don't let him."

"I don't give a fuck if he gets nervous or not. What is this, a fucking psychiatrist's office? Next time I find him like this, I'm going to kick him right in the head, and you too, got me?"

"I got you, sergeant."

"You stupid fuck, Ginsberg."

Mazursky crawled by Ginsberg and made his way to his anti-tank squad, which consisted of three anti-tank guns. He was supposed to have four, but the other one had been put out of action in the Hurtgen Forest nine days ago. The three gun crews had their ammunition ready and were poised for action.

"We might get some light tanks and some personnel carriers coming at us, so make every shot count, got me?"

"Yes sergeant."

Mazursky crawled back to the position he'd had beside Corporal Dooley, while Albright crawled right behind him.

"See anything up here?" Mazursky asked Dooley.

"Who's looking?"

"You're supposed to be looking, you stupid fuck."

"I ain't putting my head up there while these shells are falling."

"I'm surrounded by assholes." Mazursky looked at Albright. "Have you heard anything from headquarters yet?"

"If I did I would've told you."

"Just give me a yes or a no, Albright. Never mind the song and dance."

"No, sergeant."

"That's better."

Mazursky sat down in the trench. He threw away his cigar stub because it was too short to relight. He might burn his nose off. Reaching into a pocket of his field jacket, he pulled out another cigar. His mother sent him a box of them every month from East Seventh Street in New York City. Mazursky lit it and wished he was on Eighth Avenue where all the whores were.

Looking at his watch, he sat that it was 0545 hours. The bombardment had been underway for about fifteen minutes. He wondered when the attack would begin.

"Nowicki!" he yelled down the trench. "You got that BAR together yet!"

"Yes sergeant!"

"You stupid fuck," Mazursky muttered, opening the chamber of his M-1 and looking inside at the clip of .30 caliber bullets.

It's going to be a shitty day, he thought.

Chapter Two

LIEUTENANT SMITH SLID INTO THE TRENCH beside the command bunker. He readjusted his helmet, brushed mud off the front of his field jacket, and removed the ammunition clip from his carbine. Pfc. Stein landed beside him, his two little eyes peering out from underneath his helmet.

"You wait for me here, Stein."

"Yes sir."

"Keep your head down."

"Yes sir."

Lieutenant Smith opened the door of the command bunker and went inside. Captain DiPietro, a short swarthy man in helmet and Ike jacket, stood before a map on a table beneath a lantern. With him was Lieutenant Shanahan, the executive officer, Lieutenant LeDoux of the fourth platoon, Lieutenant Kingsbury of the third platoon, and Sergeant Neff of the first platoon, whose lieutenant had been felled by a machine gun burst in the Hurtgen Forest.

Smith approached the table and saluted. "Lieutenant Smith reporting, sir."

Captain DiPietro saluted back. "How's everything out your way?"

"Heavy shelling."

"Lose any men?"

"Not yet."

"Good." DiPietro scanned their faces. "Now that you're all here, we can begin." He looked at the map. "Our entire front in the Ardennes is under heavy bombardment. We don't know where the Germans got the artillery; we suspect it might have come from their Eastern Front. Anyway, we always thought that before the Germans acknowledged final defeat they'd attempt one last desperate counteroffensive. It seems likely that they have such an attack underway right now. It was through this same region that they launched their great attack of 1940 which drove the British forces from Europe and defeated the French. That attack was led by General Von Rundstedt, and we have reason to believe he's leading this attack. We cannot permit him to succeed again. Unfortunately, we're weak in this area, so we'll have to permit slight penetrations in our line as we fall back to more secure defensive positions and await the arrival of reinforcements from the rear. Then we'll push them back to Germany." He pointed to the map. "This is our position right now." He pointed to another spot. "This will be our new position, right outside the town of Dillendorf. We'll be leaving at 0630 hours. Except for the second platoon."

Lieutenant Smith thought he'd misunderstood something. "Did you say all except for the second platoon?"

"That's right, Lieutenant. Your platoon has been

chosen for a special mission of supreme importance. You've got to fight a rearguard action here." DiPietro pointed to the road that led to Dillendorf. "We expect German tanks to start moving down this road as soon as their troops secure the territory. Those tanks must be delayed so that we can retreat and regroup; otherwise they'll chew the regiment to shreds. You've got to hold them until noon."

"How many tanks will there be?"

"A panzer division."

"A panzer division? How can one platoon hold a panzer division?"

"The same way the Greeks held the pass at Thermopylae against a numerically superior force. At this point here," he pointed to the map, "the road narrows between two sizable hills that the tanks can't negotiate. In other words, they'll have to come on the road. There are cliffs and caves in the hills, and you'll set up positions in them. You'll be reinforced by an anti-tank squad from the weapons platoon. If you can knock out the lead enemy tanks, you'll block the road to them. Then you'll keep them pinned down with mortar and small arms fire so they can't get those tanks out of the way. You've got to hold them until noon."

"But sir, that's a job for a unit at least the size of a company."

"We need all the forces we can get for the defense of Dillendorf, because if the enemy gets our oil reserves there, they'll be much more dangerous."

"Doesn't it make more sense to try to stop them on the road?"

"They can't be stopped on the road. They can only be

slowed down. The road is very narrow there. A platoon should be able to do it."

"But they'll bring in artillery. They'll blow those hills away."

"Just hold them until noon."

"And then what?"

"Then you retreat to the Dillendorf defensive line."

"But we'll never be able to get out of there!"

"You must do your best, Lieutenant. That's an order."

"Yes sir."

"That's all," DiPietro said. "Return to your units and pass on the orders. Platoons one, three, and four will pull out at 0630 hours. The second platoon, augmented by the anti-tank squad from the fourth platoon, will pull out immediately. Any questions?"

No one said anything.

"You're all dismissed, except for Lieutenant Smith. Good luck, men."

"Thank you, sir."

Lieutenants LeDoux and Kingsbury and Sergeant Neff, left the command bunker.

Lieutenant Smith looked down at the map. He was six feet two and towered over Captain DiPietro.

"You'd better get out your map," DiPietro said, "and mark down the spot we want you to hold."

"Yes sir."

Smith took out his map as the artillery bombardment thundered around them. He marked the hills and worked out an azimuth to them from his present position.

"I'm sorry it has to be this way, Lieutenant," Captain DiPietro said.

"So am I." Smith folded the map back into his shirt pocket.

"Orders are orders."

"I understand."

"I didn't want to say anything in front of the others."

Smith set his jaw. "It's a suicide mission, but I guess fifteen hundred men are more important than forty."

"I'm afraid that's true."

"I just wish I weren't one of the forty."

"You are. My advice is to surrender if you make it until noon."

"We might not make it until noon."

"You have to."

"Well, we'll try." He put on his helmet. "I guess I'd better get moving." He threw a snappy salute at Captain DiPietro.

DiPietro saluted him back just as snappily, then held out his hand. "Good luck, Lieutenant."

"Thank you sir."

"Is there anything you'd like me to do?"

"If I don't make it back, it'd be nice if you wrote a personal letter to my wife."

"You can rely on it."

"Thank you sir."

Smith turned and marched out of the command bunker. Outside, Stein was waiting with his walkie-talkie.

"Everything okay, Lieutenant?" Stein asked hopefully.

"No."

"What's wrong?"

"Follow me. We're going back to our position."

DOOM PLATOON

"Yes sir."

Lieutenant Smith climbed over the side of the trench and crawled toward the second platoon trench. There were huge craters in the ground and fallen twisted trees everywhere. The air smelled like gunpowder and a mist was rising off the snow as dawn broke in the east, where the Germans were. He felt a little numb, as if he were partly dead already. He never realized that his military career would end like this.

At West Point he'd dreamed of becoming a general some day, but ever since D-Day he'd accepted that he'd probably never survive this war. The attrition rate among new lieutenants was very high. They led troops on the front lines and enemy sharpshooters picked them off easily. All the ceremony and bullshit at West Point existed to give young officers the courage and fanaticism to lead their men into machine gun fire and artillery bombardments. If you could make it to Major you'd probably never get killed, but in wartime you were lucky if you could make it until tomorrow. After D-Day he stopped thinking about becoming a general and concentrated instead on staying alive and keeping his platoon out of danger as best he could. But now he had to lead them and himself into the jaws of hell.

He slid down the side of the trench and made his way to Mazursky, who was puffing a cigar and looking morose.

"We're pulling out," Smith said. "Notify the men to get ready."

"Where we going?"

"To the Dillendorf road."

"How far back?"

"Not very far. We'll be moving almost directly to our left flank. We've got to hold the road against some tanks."

"You mean the whole regiment is going to hold the road."

"No, just the second platoon."

Mazursky's jaw dropped open and his cigar fell out of his mouth. "Huh?"

"You heard me."

"Just this platoon?"

"That's right."

"How come?"

Lieutenant Smith wondered whether or not to tell Mazursky the truth, then decided he'd better. Mazursky was an old combat veteran and a Regular Army soldier. Mazursky would know how to handle the situation.

Smith leaned toward Mazursky and said softly. "It's a rearguard action so that the regiment can get away."

"But what about us?"

"It doesn't look too good for us."

"You mean..." Mazursky's face crumbled.

"That's what I mean."

"Holy shit."

"We'll have a strong defensive position in some cliffs and caves, and we'll have the antitank squad from the weapons platoon. It won't be so bad."

"The second platoon and the anti-tank squad against tanks? How many tanks?"

" A panzer division."

Mazursky's eyes goggled. "A PANZER DIVISION!"

"Not so loud. I don't want to scare the others."

"But we won't have a fucking chance."

"Well, there's always a chance."

"But it's a suicide mission."

"That's what I told Captain DiPietro. He wished us luck."

"That cocksucker. Where's he gonna be?"

"Defending the oil dump at Dillendorf with the rest of the division. The orders have come down from headquarters. It's not his fault."

"Why'd he have to pick the second platoon? Why not the third platoon, or the first platoon?"

"Because we're the best platoon."

Mazursky shook his head. "Oh this fucking rotten war. The better you are, the more likely that you'll get a bullet in your ass."

"There's always a chance that we won't get a bullet in our ass."

"Bullshit."

"What was that, sergeant?"

"Nothing, sir."

"Tell the men to get ready to move out. I want you to take the point."

"Yes sir."

Mazursky crawled down the trench, telling the men to drop their cocks and grab their socks because they were going to move out.

"Where we going, Sarge?" asked Private Morelli, who was eighteen years old.

"If I told you, you still wouldn't know. Saddle up and get ready to move out."

"Yes, sergeant."

At the end of the trench Mazursky found Nowicki the BAR man reading a letter from home. Mazursky knew what the letter contained, because Nowicki had received it a month ago and had been reading it over and over again ever since, complaining about it to anyone who listened. The sum and substance of the letter was that Shirley, Nowicki's girlfriend, was breaking their engagement because she had found another boyfriend, a 4-F welder who earned a hundred bucks a week.

"Put away that fucking letter and get ready to move out, you scumbag," Mazursky growled at Nowicki.

"Yes sergeant," Nowicki replied forlornly, folding the letter.

Mazursky felt a rare twinge of pity for Nowicki, who was clearly a psycho case, as evidenced by his compulsive cleaning of his BAR, and his compulsive reading of Shirley's letter. Mazursky slapped his hand on Nowicki's shoulder.

"Forget about her," Mazursky said consolingly. "She's a no-good cunt and you should consider yourself lucky to be rid of her."

"But I love her," Nowicki replied pathetically.

"Love is bullshit. It's a kind of mental disease. What you need is a trip to a good whorehouse. Next time we go on pass I'll personally take you to a good whorehouse. I'll get one French whore to suck your dick and another one to stick her tongue up your ass, and by the time they're finished with you, you won't even know who you are, never mind who Shirley is."

"But she's so pretty, sergeant. She's the prettiest girl I've ever seen."

"You really think so?"

"Yes, sergeant."

"Do me a favor, will you?"

"Sure, sergeant."

"Imagine her taking a big smelly shit in the morning."

Nowicki wrinkled his big hooked nose. "Ugh!"

"Or better yet, imagine her blowing some guy in an alleyway, which is probably what she's doing right now."

Nowicki closed his eyes tightly. "Oh God!"

"Pretty picture, ain't it?" Mazursky asked, grinning like a monkey.

"Shirley wouldn't do such a thing!"

"Sure she would. Any douche bag would. They're all no fucking good. You know what you ought to do, Nowicki? You ought to do everything you can to get through this war alive, and then go back to Pittsburgh and beat that bitch's brains out. And when you get finished with her, you could kick her boyfriend's ass."

"I couldn't do that, sergeant," Nowicki said, looking forlorn again.

"That's because you're a fucking asshole. Saddle up and get ready to move out."

"Yes sergeant."

On his way back to Lieutenant Smith, Mazursky chewed his unlit cigar and thought of Sally Mae, the little waitress he'd met during a weekend pass in London. What a cute little bitch she'd been. They'd had a fantastic night together, even did it in the bathtub. He wondered who she was in the bathtub with right now. What a depraved little bitch. You'd never know it to look at her, because she was kind of shy and mousey, but get her alone and watch out. His dick had been sore for four days afterwards. When he went ashore on Omaha Beach it started hurting again when it hit that salty, oily water. He had to fight for his life on the beach with a sore dick. It hadn't been one of his better days. But he missed Sally Mae anyways. He'd sure like to see her again.

Moving toward Lieutenant Smith, Mazursky saw the men putting on their packs. He tightened a strap here and adjusted a belt there, smacking the men on the shoulders, trying to put them in the mood for the little operation dreamed up by headquarters. Mazursky hated headquarters and all those fancy officers walking around with swagger sticks, having fantasies about being great military strategists. Those assholes would get heart attacks if they had to spend more than five minutes on the front lines, but they were sending the second platoon to almost certain annihilation.

Somehow Mazursky couldn't accept the fact that he might die. Deep down, he thought he was too smart to die. He'd been in situations where men had dropped like flies all around him, and yet somehow he came through with only minor injuries. Somewhere out there he knew there was a bullet with his name on it, but he was confident that somehow he'd be able to dodge it. Why would he be able to dodge it? Because I ain't an asshole like everybody else, that's why.

Lieutenant Smith was at the end of the trench with a group of faces Mazursky recognized as belonging to the anti-tank squad from the weapons platoon. They were led by Corporal Dahl, an Irishman with wide hips and narrow shoulders, who hailed from the Yorkville section of Manhattan, about seventy blocks from where Mazurksy's mother lived.

"Hiya Dahl."

"Whataya say, Mazursky."

"Not much."

Lieutenant Smith cleared his throat. "Are the men ready to move out, sergeant?"

"Yes sir."

"You take the first squad and move them out in a column of ducks in that direction." Lieutenant Smith pointed toward the northeast.

"Column of ducks, sir?"

"Yes. That way we'll always present a skirmish line to the enemy."

"What if we run into enemy troops that're in front of us, or behind us, or anywhere except where they're supposed to be?"

"We'll adjust our flanks accordingly."

"What if we're surrounded?"

"We'll get into diamond formations."

"Then why not leave in diamond formations in the first place, with the anti-tank squad and you in the center?"

"It'll be slower that way."

"Not that much slower, but it'll be a lot safer. Remember what happened in the Hurtgen Forest."

"Okay, move them out in diamonds, with the first squad on point. You take the first squad, and stay in touch over the walkie-talkie, got it?"

"Yes sir."

Mazursky turned around and, in the dawn, saw the trench full of dirty bedraggled soldiers looking at him.

"Where's Fuckbright?" he asked.

Albright stepped out of the row of soldiers. "Here I am, sergeant."

"Follow me, Fuckbright. And keep your ear glued to your walkie-talkie."

"Hup, Sarge."

"Hup Sarge? Where in the fuck do you think you are, in boot camp? Just give me a plain yes or no from now on, understand?"

"Hup Sarge. I mean yes."

"You fucking birdbrain!"

"Yes, sergeant."

German shells were still raining down on the Charlie Company area as Mazursky shouldered his way to the center of the trench. "All right you assholes," he yelled, "we're moving out in four diamond formations, with the anti-tank squad in the center. I'll be in the point squad, and Lieutenant Smith will be with the anti-tank squad. Keep your eyes open and your fucking asses close to the ground. Squad leaders will stay in touch on their walkie-talkies. Any questions?"

"What happened to breakfast?" asked Private Naughton of Boston.

Mazursky glowered at him. " You fat fuck, all you ever think about is food! We'll have breakfast when we get to where we're going! Any other questions?"

Nobody dared ask anything.

"Okay—move 'em out!"

Mazursky crawled to the extreme left flank of the trench where Corporal Ginsberg's first squad was deployed. "Okay boys, up and at 'em!" Mazursky yelled.

Pfc. Miguel Nazario was point man for the squad. He scrambled up the side of the trench, fell into a shell crater, and then began hunching his way across no-man's land. Next came Privates Winchell and Brouvelli, who took positions on Nazario's flanks, several feet behind him. Then the two BAR men went out, Privates Nowicki and Johnson, who would be farthest out on the flanks. Finally Mazursky, Albright, Ginsberg, and the last four men crawled out of the trench and took positions so that if the squad could be seen from above, it would look like a diamond moving across the terrain. The other squads would also form similar diamonds, positioning themselves overall so that the platoon itself would look like a large diamond made of five smaller diamonds. This would, as Mazursky pointed out earlier, provide a fairly effective all-round security.

The second platoon moved across the shell craters and broken trees. Whenever an incoming shell sounded like it might land close, they dropped to their bellies on the snow and prayed that it wouldn't fall on them. After the shell exploded they got up and kept moving.

Mazursky's eyes were darting about at trees, boulders, gullies, looking for signs of enemy troop movements. In the distance where the enemy lines were he could make out the rumble of a bombardment, which meant that the allied artillery was retaliating. Good. Bomb the bastards into smithereens. They came to a little valley in the woodland area and went down into it. It was a peaceful little valley that somehow, miraculously, had escaped the shellfire. Through its center passed a little brook. Mazursky marveled at how peaceful the little valley was; it was hard for him to imagine that there was a war on. And then he realized that there'd been no shelling for the past several minutes.

Lieutenant Smith, at the center of the antitank squad, also was aware that the shelling had stopped. He didn't consider this good news, because it meant that the German troop attack would begin now, and after that the panzer division would show up on the road to Dillendorf. Turning to Stein, he told him to call Mazursky on the walkie-talkie.

"Mazursky here."

"This is Lieutenant Smith. Have you noticed that the shelling has stopped."

"Yes sir. I was just about to call you and tell you so."

"We'll be able to move faster now. Tell the men to step it out."

"Yes-sir."

Mazursky handed the walkie-talkie back to Albright. "All right you cocksuckers!" he yelled. "They ain't shelling us anymore so move your fucking asses—let's go!"

They went up the side of the valley and found themselves in a sparsely wooded plain. Mazursky looked at his watch; it was 0715 hours but still fairly dark because of the thick blanket of clouds. He chewed his cigar stub and searched for signs of the enemy. There was nothing that he could see.

They crossed the plain and entered a thickly wooded forest. The branches and bushes slowed them down and scratched their faces. The day became a bit brighter, but there was still too much cloud cover for air support. From afar, Mazursky could hear the sound of bombardments, machine gun fire, and small arms fire. Battles seemed to be going on everywhere. He looked ahead and saw Nazario threading his way through the bushes.

"Lieutenant Smith wants to talk to you, sergeant," said Albright, holding out the walkie-talkie.

Mazursky took the walkie-talkie and pressed the button. "Mazursky here."

"This is Lieutenant Smith, sergeant. Tell the men to take a break in place, and I want you to report to me immediately."

"Yes sir."

Mazursky handed back the walkie-talkie and held out his arms, the signal to stop. Then he waved his arms, the signal to get down. Around him, the second platoon dropped to the snow.

"Corporal Dooley!"

"Hup Sarge!"

"Get over here!"

"Hup Sarge!"

Dooley came crawling from the rear of the first squad diamond, his M-1 cradled in his arms.

"Take charge of your squad," Mazursky told him. "I've gotta go back and talk to Lieutenant Smith."

"Gotcha."

Mazursky turned to Albright. "Stay close."

"Hup Sarge."

"I thought I told you to cut that 'Hup Sarge' shit out."

"How come you didn't say anything when Corporal Dooley said it?"

Mazursky squinted his eyes. "Have you somehow without me knowing it become promoted over me, Fuckbright?"

"No, sergeant."

"Then who in the fuck are you to ask me why I say things and why I don't?"

"I don't know, Sarge."

"Then hereafter keep your asshole questions to yourself, understand?"

"Hup Sarge."

Mazursky grabbed him by the throat. "You little shitfucker, I'm going to kill you if you don't cut that out!"

"I'm sorry sergeant—I forgot!" Albright squealed.

"You'd better not forget again."

"I won't. I won't."

Mazursky let him go. "Now follow me."

"Yes, Sergeant Mazursky."

"That's better."

Mazursky raised his head and looked around. The second platoon was lying on the snow or the portions of the ground that were bare. In the distance he could see nothing. He leapt to his feet and ran in a crouch to the center of the anti-tank diamond, which happened to be right behind the first squad diamond. He heard Albright running behind him. Bursting past the point man of anti-tank squad, he headed for Lieutenant Smith and dropped on his belly beside him. A second later Albright dropped behind him. Mazursky hoped everybody in the platoon had seen his own little run, so that they'd realize he was still in good physical shape and could kick ass if that became necessary.

"At ease, sergeant."

"Yes, sir."

"Take out your notepad, pencil, compass, and map, please."

"Yes, sir."

Mazursky removed the required objects from his pockets, as Lieutenant Smith spread his own map out on his poncho.

"I thought I'd better tell you our exact line of march and our objective," Lieutenant Smith said. He pointed to the map. "This is where we are now." He pointed to a spot on the Dillendorf road. "And this is where were going. Mark it on your map."

"Yes, sir." Mazursky made the mark.

"We're on an azimuth of about 270 degrees. Write it down."

"Yes, sir." Mazursky wrote it down.

"There are cliffs and caves at our objective on the road. That's where we make our stand. You got that?"

"Yes, sir."

"Good. You may return to your squad now."

"Yes, sir."

"Give them another five minutes of rest and then move them out."

"Yes, sir."

"And keep your eyes peeled."

"Yes, sir."

Mazursky and Albright ran back to their position in the first squad and dropped to their stomachs. They rested another five minutes, and then Mazursky got to his feet. The platoon members saw him and knew the break was over. Grumbling, they got up. Mazursky moved his arm over his head and they moved out again.

In their diamond formations, the second platoon continued moving through the forest. On the other side was a hill that they went around, and then there was a farmer's field. Mazursky figured that the Dillendorf Road must be less than a mile away. They passed over the field and entered some gently rolling wooded hills.

A shot rang out, and Private Nazario fell like a sack of potatoes.

"HIT IT!" screamed Mazursky.

The second platoon dove to the ground as the crackle of rifle shots filled the forest. Bullets zipped over their heads. Mazursky raised his head an inch off the ground and peered underneath his helmet at the woods. He heard the sound of a machine gun. They didn't sound too far away and they didn't seem like there were very many of them. Evidently they only had one machine gun. If they had a tank they would have used it by now. Looking at the woods ahead he saw flashes of light and puffs of smoke. There weren't very many of them. Probably it was just a patrol. A figure stood up and threw something. It landed near the second square and exploded—a hand grenade.

The right flanks of the first and second squads opened

fire on the enemy patrol. Mazursky could hear the put-put-put of Nowicki's BAR. Nowicki was a stupid fuck, but he knew what to do with a BAR. His tracers whizzed into the enemy patrol, so everybody else could see where they were. Then the riflemen began firing.

Albright nudged Mazursky. "Lieutenant Smith wants you."

Mazursky took the walkie-talkie. "Yeah?"

"Form a skirmish line with the first, second, and third squad. I don't think there are very many of them. We can't afford to get pinned down here. We'll have to attack. Wait for my order."

"Yes, sir."

Mazursky handed back the walkie-talkie. He rammed a round into the chamber of his M-1 and looked up to see Private Johnson throw a hand grenade. It landed in a bush, exploded, and a German soldier minus an arm and a leg went flying into the air.

"SKIRMISH LINE!" yelled Mazursky. "SQUADS ONE TWO THREE!"

The three squads, their battle-tested soldiers firing all the time, moved into a skirmish line against the Germans. Mazursky ran to the left of the line, dropped, and began crawling down its length, positioning the men.

"You move over a few feet, Mazzoli! Hey, Krupsak, fire that motherfucking BAR! What do you think it's for? Move up there, Ginsberg! Get your ass down, Dooley! Fire that fucking rifle, Collins!"

Private Larry Collins, of North Platte, Nebraska, didn't move.

"I said fire that fucking rifle, Collins!"

Collins still didn't move.

Mazursky crawled to him and batted him on the shoulder. "What the fuck's wrong with you!"

Collins didn't respond. He just lay there with his head in his helmet. Mazursky raised Collins's shoulder a few inches, and Collins's helmet fell away. So did half of Collins's face. It had been shot away, and Mazursky stared in horror at the steaming bloody brains. The stench like a freshly broiled steak. Mazursky wanted to throw up. He swallowed hard and continued down the line to the midway point, then tucked his rifle into his shoulder, took aim, and squeezed off a round at something that moved behind a bush. A German soldier screamed and fell forward, clutching a hole in his gut.

Corporal Dooley pulled the pin out of a hand grenade and hurled it at the German machine gun nest. It landed near where the machine guns were firing, there was an explosion, and three mangled German bodies went flying into the air. Dooley smiled, and the smile suddenly became an ugly grimace as a German bullet smashed into his forehead. His hand dropped into the snow. The war was over for Dooley.

The second platoon continued pouring bullets and hand grenades into the German patrol. The German fire became progressively more sporadic.

"FIX BAYONETS!" screamed Lieutenant Smith.

Mazursky pulled his bayonet from his scabbard and fixed it to the end of his M-1. Nervously he chewed the stub of his cigar. He wasn't too crazy about bayonet attacks. Anything could go wrong.

"CHARGE!" yelled Lieutenant Smith.

Mazursky leapt to his feet. "UP AND AT 'EM!"

Mazursky ran toward the enemy line, carrying his rifle in his left hand. In his right hand was a hand grenade with the pin already pulled. His knuckles were white over the lever that activated the firing mechanism. Behind him on both sides he heard the rumbling feet of the second platoon. He heard rebel yells, hee-haws, and blood-curdling screams. Bullets whizzed all around them. Somebody to his right yelped and went crashing to the ground. Mazursky huffed and puffed as the enemy line drew closer. His eyes scanned back and forth. To his left two German soldiers in the black uniforms of the Waffen SS got up from behind a lot. Mazursky threw the hand grenade at them and dropped to the ground.

"HIT IT!" he shouted.

The hand grenade exploded. Mazursky jumped to his feet again.

"FOLLOW ME! KILL THE COCKSUC-KERS!"

Mazursky held his cigar stub tight into his teeth as he ran into the smoke of the grenade blast. The two German SS soldiers were blown all over the vicinity. In a bush behind them another German stood up, a Luger in one of his hands and an entrenching tool in the other. The fucker was ready for hand-to-hand combat. Mazursky fired from the hip and the German went flying backwards, a red hole in his chest. Looking to his left and right, Mazursky saw the men of the second platoon grappling hand to hand with the remnants of the German patrol. He kept advancing forward and then from behind a tree came a German soldier, not more than seventeen years, his rifle and bayonet at the ready.

Before Mazursky could fire a round the German yelled a battle cry and charged, the point of his bayonet streaking toward Mazursky's heart. Mazursky cursed and parried the lunge, bringing the butt of his rifle around in the same motion and slamming it against the side of the German's head. The German boy went down, blood running out of his ears. Mazursky bent over and jabbed the point of his bayonet through the German's heart.

He heard something close by. Looking up, he saw a big German soldier coming at him with his rifle and bayonet. Mazursky knew he didn't have time to pull his bayonet out of the German on the ground and defend himself. He was completely defenseless. It was all over. Then there was a shot, and the German's jaw disappeared. He fell to a clump on the ground at Mazursky's feet. Mazursky turned around to see who fired the shot, and saw Albright grinning, his cheek against the butt of his carbine.

It was about time that asshole made himself useful, Mazursky thought as he moved deeper into the woods with his rifle at port arms. To his right there was movement. A black uniform was running through the woods. Mazursky raised his M-1, sighted down his bloody bayonet blade, and pulled the trigger. The black uniform went spinning against a tree, and then slid down to the ground.

Another German soldier jumped up from behind the stump of a tree. He had his rifle and bayonet ready, and terror was in his eyes.

"FUCK YOU!" Mazursky bellowed as he lunged forward.

The German deftly parried Mazursky's bayonet, and Mazursky's forward motion brought him face to face with the German. He could smell the German's foul breath and see the pimple on his nose. The German pushed hard, and Mazursky went sprawling backwards, but kept his rifle solid in his grip. He lunged forward again quickly, and this time the German wasn't fast enough to parry him. The blade of Mazursky's bayonet punched through the German's black tunic, and blood poured out. The German's eyes rolled back into his head as his knees buckled. Mazursky yanked out his bayonet, and blood spurted onto Mazursky's sleeves, for he'd severed a main artery near the German's heart. The German fell in a heap to the ground.

Mazursky looked around excitedly. He saw no movement, and the forest was becoming still again. Moving backwards, he encountered the men of the second platoon and their victims sprawled all over the ground. Some of the Americans were going through the pockets of the Germans, stealing watches, money, and medals. Private Rubin of the second squad was sporting a Luger he'd taken from the body of a German officer he'd shot between the eyes. Private Harris of the 1st squad was struggling to pull his bayonet out of the rib cage of a German sergeant, where it was stuck.

"Pull the fucking trigger," Mazursky said.

Private Harris pulled the trigger, and the German's body blew apart. The bayonet came out easily, because there was nothing holding it anymore.

"Thanks, Sarge," said Private Harris.

"You fucking asshole.'

Mazursky walked throughout the battle area, surveying the damage. The second platoon had lost four men in the bayonet fight. Mazursky chewed his cigar and cursed under his breath. The second platoon couldn't afford to lose any more men.

Pfc. Stein stumbled toward Mazursky, a hangdog look on his face. "He's dead," he murmured.

"Who's dead?" Mazursky asked.

"Lieutenant Smith."

"He is!"

"See for yourself." Stein pointed behind a bush.

Mazursky stomped into the bush and saw Lieutenant Smith lying behind it. Smith's face was even paler than usual, his eyes were closed, and his mouth was open. He looked as though he was asleep. His straight blond hair lay over his forehead. He was 27 years old. And the snow around his stomach was drenched with his blood.

Mazursky knelt beside him and turned him over onto his back. He felt for Smith's pulse, and there was none. He bent over and listened to his heart to make sure, and there was no beat. Stein hadn't been mistaken; Smith was truly dead. Deader than a doornail. Mazursky was now platoon leader. The next ranking man would have been Corporal Dooley, but he was dead too. That meant Corporal Banes of the third squad was the new platoon sergeant. If he was alive.

Mazursky looked at Pfc. Stein, who was sobbing softly. "What the fuck's wrong with you, asshole!"

"Nothing sergeant."

"Go get me Corporal Banes, if he's still alive. If he's not, get me Corporal Ginsberg."

"What if he's not alive either?"

"We'll worry about that then."

Stein ran off, and Mazursky bent over Lieutenant Smith again. Smith had been a pretty good lieutenant, as lieutenants go. Mazursky took off Smith's dog tags and put them into his pants pocket. Then he took Smith's carbine and ammunition; he'd always wanted to carry a carbine because they were lighter than an M-1. Now, as the new platoon leader he was entitled to carry it. He took out Smith's maps, compass, and wallet. One of these days, he'd send the wallet to Smith's next of kin. Providing he lived that long. He would have liked to give Smith a decent burial, but there was no time for that.

Stein returned with Corporal Banes, a tall, lanky, Texan. Mazursky stood up.

"You know who this is on the ground here?" Mazursky asked.

"It looks like Lieutenant Smith."

"That's right. He's dead. I'm the new platoon leader. And you're the new acting platoon sergeant. You know what a platoon sergeant's supposed to do?"

"Whatever the platoon leader says."

"Right. Don't ever forget it. I want you to follow whatever order I give you, no matter what. I will put up with no back talk at all. This is war and I got a right to put a fucking bullet through your head if you give me any trouble. Get it?"

"Got it."

"Kneel down here. I want to show you something."

They kneeled beside the stiffening corpse of Lieutenant Smith. Mazursky spread Smith's map on the ground and explained their mission on the Dillendorf Road. Corporal Banes listened with mounting disbelief.

"Did you say we're gonna have to stall a panzer division?" Banes asked.

"That's what I said."

"But that's impossible!"

"Who in the fuck asked you for your opinion?"

"But it's fucking crazy."

"It's an order. And we're going to carry it out. Understand?"

"Yeah."

"What do you mean, yeah?"

"Yes, sergeant."

"That's better. Take this map and compass. If anything happens to me, it's your platoon and your mission. Where's Stein?"

"I'm right here, sergeant," said Stein, his bazooka and walkie-talkie hanging from his shoulders. He was a frail little man who somehow had a considerable amount of stamina.

"Stein, from now on you're Corporal Banes' runner. He's the new acting platoon sergeant, got it?"

"But I'm supposed to be the platoon leader's runner, not the platoon sergeant's," Stein protested meekly.

Mazursky glared at him. "What was that?"

Stein looked at the ground. "Nothing, sergeant."

Albright was standing nearby, a skinny pickle from Cleveland, grinning.

"What the fuck's so funny?" Mazursky asked him.

"Nothing, sergeant."

"Then wipe that stupid asshole smile off your face."

"Yes, sergeant."

Mazursky looked at Banes and narrowed his eyes to slits. Banes had a lantern jaw, an aquiline nose, and his eyes were pale blue.

"I'm gonna stay with the point squad," Mazursky said. "You take Lieutenant Smith's post with the anti-tank squad. Keep your fucking eyes open and stay awake. Get the men ready to move out."

"Yes, sergeant." Banes adjusted the M-1 slung over his right shoulder and walked away. "FALL IN!" he shouted.

Mazursky looked down at Lieutenant Smith, who looked like a teenage boy. It was strange how dead soldiers always looked like little boys. In a few weeks Mrs. Smith would get a telegram from the Department of the Army. It would say that her husband had been killed in action. Mazursky wondered how she'd take it.

He trudged to the first squad. The men carried more junk than before; they'd taken ammunition and C-rations from their dead. Nobody had to give them the order to do that. The good thing about combat veterans was that they generally knew what to do. The bad thing was that they cared more about saving their own skins than taking military objectives. Mazursky wondered how they'd react when they saw a German panzer division headed straight for them.

He took his position at the center of the first squad and looked around. Albright was behind him, and the other squads were in their diamond formations. He took out his compass and faced the 270-degree azimuth that was supposed to take them to their defensive position on the Dillendorf road. Then he raised his right hand over his head and pointed in that direction.

The second platoon moved out. They passed through the gently rolling hills and came to another meadow. There was a bombed out farmhouse and a barn that, miraculously, hadn't been touched. It was that way with troops too. A hand grenade could blow four men into little pieces of meat, and the fifth man wouldn't have a scratch on him. What a crazy fucking war.

When Mazursky enlisted in 1935, he didn't know there was going to be a war. He thought he was going to put twenty easy years in the Army and then retire on a pension that would amount to two-thirds of his base salary. He did all right for three years, but then in the beginning of his second enlistment he started boozing it up. There'd been a fight in Wrightstown, New Jersey, just outside of Fort Dix. Some corporal from the 101st Airborne cracked wise with him, and Mazursky nearly beat him to death. That produced his first court martial. There'd been three others since then. But those fucking paratroopers were always too cocky for their own good. Thought they were some kind of elite, just because they were dumb enough to jump out of airplanes. But he'd shown that fucking corporal a thing or two. That corporal would probably have headaches for the rest of his life. At least Mazursky hoped he would.

DOOM PLATOON

Private Winfield, the new point man, pointed his finger to his left. Mazursky looked and saw something walking toward him over the snow. It was a little dog, about the size of a cocker spaniel. The dog was wagging his tail so hard the entire rear of his body was wagging with it. The dog walked up to Private Nowicki, stood on its hind legs, and pawed the air. Nowicki shrugged and kept on walking. Undaunted, the dog headed for Mazursky It was white with black spots, a mongrel of some kind, and had a black spot around its right eye which made it appear that he had a shiner. He was so skinny you could see every one of its ribs.

The dog walked beside Mazursky, wagging its tail, and looked up mournfully at him.

"What the fuck do you want?"

The dog kept walking and wagging.

Mazursky looked back at Albright. "Take a can of sausage patties out of my pack, open it, and give it to the mutt."

"Hup Sarge."

"WHAT!"

"Sorry, sergeant. Yes, sergeant."

"You fucking stupid ridiculous bolo cocksucker!"

As Mazursky continued walking, Albright ran closer, opened Mazursky's pack, took out the can of C-rations, and opened it up. Then he stopped, emptied the can onto the snow, and buried the can. The dog began to gulp down the patties. Mazursky glanced back, wishing he were that dog. A dog didn't have to carry a rifle. A dog didn't have to stick a bayonet into anybody. A dog wouldn't have to fight off a panzer division until noon.

The second platoon moved into another stand of trees.

He heard the pitter-patter of tiny feet, looked down, and saw the dog walking beside him. The fucking dog thought he'd found a friend. The trouble with friends was that sometimes they got killed before your eyes.

"Get the fuck out of here!" Mazursky growled at the dog.

The dog kept walking beside him.

Mazursky stamped his foot on the ground. "I said beat it!"

The dog stopped, looked sadly at him, then continued walking.

"Okay, it's your funeral," Mazursky muttered.

They continued moving through the woods. Mazursky thought the road couldn't be too far off, unless they were on the wrong azimuth and hopelessly off. It'd happened before to the second platoon. Mazursky had never met anybody who could be deadly accurate with those field compasses. Once during maneuvers at Fort Benning, Georgia a whole company had got lost for 48 hours. Today that company commander was probably peeling potatoes in some crazy mess hall someplace.

Mazursky's feet hurt and he felt hungry. He cursed the war and prayed that it would end in the next five minutes, although he knew that was impossible. His experiences since D-Day had convinced him that there would always be wars. Some greedy bastard wanted the real estate that belonged to his neighbor; that's how they always started. And you couldn't let them get away with it because then they'd want more and before you knew it they were demanding your own back yard. It was like when somebody started crowding you in a bar. If you let him get away with it he'd push you right out the front door.

A tall hill loomed up ahead. Mazursky thought it might be a good idea if he went up there and looked around. Maybe he'd see the road. He pointed toward the ground and then dropped down. The second platoon hit the snow all around him. He turned to Albright. "Tell Banes to report."

"Yes, sergeant."

Albright spoke into his walkie-talkie, and Mazursky looked at the dog lying down and wagging his tail beside him.

"You think this is fun, huh?" Mazursky asked the dog.

The dog wiggled ecstatically.

"When they start shooting at us, we'll see how long you hang around."

The dog yawned.

"I guess we might as well give you a name. From now on you're Private Shitface and you report directly to me, got it?"

The dog pawed the snow. Mazursky smiled. Maybe it was a good thing for the platoon to have a mascot. Maybe it would bring good luck. And maybe it wouldn't.

"If you ever bark when you're not supposed to, I'm gonna step right on your fucking head, got it?"

The dog stopped wagging its tail and looked seriously at Mazursky, who was flabbergasted by the thought that maybe the dog had understood him.

Banes came running, threw out the butt of his rifle, and let it cushion his fall. "You wanted me?" he asked, breathing hard.

"Yeah, I wanted you. I'm going up on that hill over

there and reconnoiter the area. You stay behind and take charge of the company. If I don't come back in fifteen minutes, proceed without me. If you see any enemy troops, don't fire at them unless they start firing first, or unless you're sure that they've seen you. Got it?"

"Can I let the men eat?"

"Can you let the men eat what?"

Banes looked away for a second. "Can I let the men eat, Sergeant?"

"That's better. No, you can't let the men eat. They'll eat when and if we set up our defensive position on the Dillendorf Road."

"They're awfully hungry, sir."

"So am I. But we can't take the time. And besides, if they're hungry, maybe they'll move a little faster. If they eat they might want to slow down and have a nap. It'll take their incentive away, got it?"

"Yes sergeant."

"If you're attacked, do you think you can handle it?"

"Yes sergeant."

"You'd fucking better, because if you don't, it's nobody's ass but your own." Mazursky turned back to Albright. "Let's go, shit-for-brains."

"Where are we going, sergeant?"

"You'll find out when we get there."

Mazursky got up, adjusted his carbine, took a chew of his unlit cigar, and stepped out toward the big hill. Albright walked to his right, and the dog to his left. After going only a short distance they could no longer see the second platoon, so thick were the woods. Mazursky's feet crunched on the frozen snow and he wished he could snuggle next to a fire someplace. After the war was over he intended to move to a warm climate. Living in the snow was getting on his nerves.

"Can I ask you something, sergeant?" Albright said.

"No."

"But it's important."

"Go ahead."

Albright looked sideways at him. He was nineteen years old, from Boston, and his face had been ravaged by acne. "I was thinking that maybe when we get back to the regiment you might put me in for corporal."

"Oh, were you really thinking that?"

"Yes, sergeant."

"Who told you that you know how to think?"

"Everybody knows how to think, sergeant."

"That's bullshit. If everybody knew how to think the world wouldn't be in the bad shape it is."

"But I've got three years in as a PFC, sergeant."

"So what? There's guys who've been a PFC longer."

"But I'm your runner. You should look out for me."

"You're wrong. You're the one who should look out for me."

"I do look out for you."

"I know. That's why I want to keep you as my runner. You're a good runner. But you might not be a good corporal."

"But sergeant, you're holding back my military career."

"What military career?"

"My military career. I been in the Army four years."

"So what? I been in for nine years."

"I should get a promotion. I do my job okay."

"That's why I want you to keep doing it."

"But I should be a squad leader by now. I got lots of experience. I been watching you operate for six months, now."

"You're lucky you're not dead by now. Count your blessings, Fuckbright."

"But now that Corporal Dooley's dead, there's a slot for another corporal. Why can't it be me?"

"You really wanna know why?"

"Yeah, I really wanna know why."

"You wanna know why what?"

"I wanna know why, sergeant."

"I'll tell you why." Mazursky looked Albright in the eye. "Because I don't think you can handle a squad. Being a corporal means more than getting another stripe and another ten dollars a month. It means you've got to be able to lead your men in battle. I don't think you could lead men in battle. Who in the fuck would want to follow your orders if the shit hits the fan? If I get busted to private again I'm liable to wind up in your squad, and let me tell you, I wouldn't be able to have much faith in you. So don't ask me about it anymore."

Albright looked hurt. "How come you wouldn't have any faith in me?"

"You're a skinny little fucked-up punk, that's why. Would you want to be in a squad commanded by an asshole like you, or would you rather be in a squad commanded by Corporal Banes?"

Albright wrinkled his forehead in thought.

"You haven't answered my question, Fuckbright."

"I'd rather be in Corporal Banes' squad," he admitted.

"Who could blame you?"

"Oh shit, sergeant."

"Stop whining, Fuckbright."

"You make me feel like shit."

"That's because you are shit. A Pfc. in this man's army is just a shit. Maybe you'd better keep that in mind."

"If a Pfc. is shit, then what's a private?"

"A private is like a piece of whale shit, and you know, there's nothing lower than whale shit, because it's right at the bottom of the ocean."

"So who's gonna be the new corporal?"

"I don't know yet. MacDoodle I think."

"MacDoodle?"

"Yeah. What's the matter with MacDoodle?"

"He's a psycho, for crying out loud! He's completely out of his mind! He's just a bloodthirsty killer! Everybody's afraid he's going to go berserk some day!"

Mazursky nodded and smiled. "And that's why they're all afraid of him, right?"

"Right."

"That's why he'll be a good squad leader. It's a very good thing to have your men afraid of you. You've got to make them more afraid of you than the enemy. Then they'll do whatever you say. Got it?"

Albright shrugged. "I think so, sergeant."

"If you stop being such a little punk candy ass, you might get to be a corporal someday. But I don't think you can do it."

"I can do it," Albright said in a deadly tone.

"Bullshit."

"You'll see."

"I don't believe in miracles anymore. I don't believe in Santa Claus either."

Albright jutted out his lower lip. "I saved your life today," he said.

Mazursky harumphed. "And it's a good thing you did, because where would you be without me, you little asshole?"

Albright couldn't think of a reply to that, because it was true, Mazursky was his god. He always felt safer when he was around Mazursky. He believed that Mazursky always knew the right thing to do. In fact, he'd had more faith in Mazursky than in Lieutenant Smith. He'd always been afraid that Lieutenant Smith would lead them into some kind of horrible situation someday, because Smith was an officer, and officers were full of shit. But Mazursky wasn't full of shit. Mazursky had a good head on his shoulders. Albright respected Mazursky more than he respected his own father, who owned a little grocery store near Copley Square and bellyached all the time. Albright's mother had run off with the salesman from a canned soup company when Albright was ten years old. Momma, why didn't you love me more than you loved that fast-talking salesman?

They came to the base of the hill and began to climb, bending forward and pulling themselves up with the help of the bare saplings that stood in the snow. The dog scampered up ahead of them. Albright was very hungry. When he'd fed the dog those sausage patties he'd wanted to steal one for himself, but if he did Mazursky might have caught him and that would've meant a kick in the ass in front of the whole platoon, or worse, a rifle butt across the snout.

"Are you paying attention?" Mazursky asked as they climbed the hill.

"Yes, sergeant."

"You don't look it."

"I can't help it how I look."

"Assholes like you worry about everything except what they're supposed to be worrying about. Pay attention, got it?"

"Yes, sergeant."

"You fucking horse's ass."

Up the hill they went, breathing hard, ever on the lookout for Germans. There were twenty-foot boulders that they had to circumnavigate and little streams that they had to jump over. Mazursky noticed that his hunger was going away. There always comes a point where a stomach gets used to being empty. That lasts for a few hours, and then when it gets hungry again you have to feed it or else get headaches and the miss-meal cramps.

Finally they reached the top of the hill. Breathing like racehorses after 12 furlongs at Belmont Park, they looked around. Straight ahead was the Dillendorf road, about half a mile away. It wound its way through forests and meadowlands. Mazursky took out his binoculars, map, and compass. He scanned the road, then looked at the map and tried to associate landmarks. He spotted the swamp that was near the hills where he was supposed to defend the road. The road turned in reality just where it turned on the map. If the second platoon had continued in the direction it was going, it only would have been a few miles off. Now he could hit the cliffs dead on. It shouldn't take more than another half hour.

Looking north on the road, he could see no traffic whatsoever. That was a good sign. In the distance he could see smoke pouring into the air above the German lines. The sound of bombardment had been going on steadily ever since 0530 hours that morning, and he'd been growing used to it. He looked at his watch; it was 0730 hours. Holding up the binoculars again, he peered through them at the woods to the north. He couldn't see anything except a thick mass of trees, and then a meadow came into view. Streams of ants were moving across the meadow, only they really weren't ants. They were Germans, at least a battalion of them, possibly two battalions.

"Oh-oh," murmured Mazursky.

"Whataya see, Sarge?"

"Give me the walkie-talkie."

Mazursky snatched it out of Albright's hands. He held it against his face and pressed the button. "Red dog one calling red dog four. Red-dog one calling red-dog four. Over."

He let go the button and listened. "Red dog four to red dog one. Red-dog four to red-dog one. Over."

"Is this Stein?" Mazursky asked.

"Yes sergeant."

"Put Corporal Banes on."

"Yes sergeant."

There was a pause.

"Banes here."

"This is Mazursky. I've just spotted a couple of battalions of krauts coming down from the north, but the road isn't too far away. We've got to move fast. Get the men off their asses and meet me at the bottom of the hill I'm on, the southern side. Got me?"

"Yes sergeant."

"You having any problems down there?"

"The men are pissed off about missing chow."

"That's tough shit. Anything else?"

"No, sergeant."

"Over and out."

Mazursky handed the walkie-talkie back to Albright. The dog was pissing against a tree.

"Follow me," Mazursky said to Albright.

They went down the side of the hill, hanging onto saplings to keep from falling. But they slipped and fell anyway, on the ice and snow. The dog was on his ass most of the way down. Mazursky took a scratch across his nose and when he touched it with his black glove he saw a little blood on his fingers. His nose stung. "Son of a bitch," he muttered. He was getting sweaty and the stink of his body rose from beneath his collar. He hadn't bathed since they arrived in the Ardennes four days ago. His balls were getting itchy. Every time he looked around he was suffering a new discomfort. "Son of a bitch!"

"You call me sergeant?"

"If I call you, you'll know about it, Fuckbright.'

They reached the bottom of the hill. The platoon hadn't arrived yet. Mazursky wiped blood off his nose and looked at Albright, who looked piqued. The dog was prancing around wagging his tail. The little fucker was having fun. Mazursky wondered what had happened to the cigar stub he'd been chewing. It must have fallen out on the way down the hill. He didn't want to put a fresh one in his mouth because he didn't have time to smoke it and it'd probably be broke in half by one of these goddamned low-hanging branches. He thought he'd be all right if only he could smoke a cigar. And he only had three of them left. He hadn't had a package from his mother in almost five weeks. The mails were fucked up again. What a fucking war.

He heard feet crunching on the snow, and dropped to his stomach. So did Albright and the dog. Mazursky pointed his carbine at the sound and rammed a round into the chamber. He flicked off the safety. Private Winfield, the point man of the first squad appeared in the mass of foliage. Sergeant Mazursky stood up. Private Winfield dropped to his stomach reflexively before he had a chance to recognize Sergeant Mazursky. The whole second platoon hit the dirt.

"Stupid fucks," Mazursky muttered as he walked back to them.

Private Winfield got up, a sheepish look on his face.

Mazursky slapped him on the shoulder. "It's okay, you did right. You should always hit the dirt first and think second. You're a good point man."

Winfield, a Kentucky farm boy, shuffled his feet like a teen-aged girl at the high school prom. Mazursky walked past him and saw Corporal Banes come crashing through the woods.

"What's up?" asked Banes.

"Form the men into two columns of ducks. We've got to double-time the fuck out of here."

DOOM PLATOON

Banes ran back, shouting orders. He lined up the first and second squads on the right and the third, fourth, and anti-tank squads on the left. The men had been at the front long enough to know that each should stay six feet behind the man in front of him.

Mazursky, followed by Albright, moved to the center of the four columns.

"DOUBLE-TIME! Mazursky shouted.

The second platoon began running through the woods. They didn't know why they were running, but they knew there must be trouble someplace. They forgot about their hunger and cold toes. They forgot about their wives and sweethearts back home. They jumped over rocks, dodged trees, and charged through bushes. There was a brook too wide to jump over so they went splashing through, the icy water biting their feet. They ran up a hill and down its other side. They ran around another hill. They slid and fell down on the ice covering a small lake. On the other side was a clump of trees, and behind the trees was the Dillendorf road.

Mazursky, running at the head of the columns, was the first to see the road. He hit the dirt, and so did the second platoon behind him. Lying still, he listened for a few moments, but heard nothing. He turned to Albright.

"You stay here."

"Yes, sergeant."

Leaving the second platoon on their stomachs in the woods, Mazursky crawled toward the road, his carbine strap wrapped around his right forearm. In the open now, in the gully beside the road, he looked to his right and left, and saw nothing. But he was too low to see if anything was coming down the road itself. He crawled up the steep gully. As his head rose to road level he moved very slowly. His big brown eyes were even with the road. There was nothing on it except tracks. Looking to the right, he saw no Germans coming. To the left, he could see nothing. So far so good. He crawled back down the gully and made his way to the woods. When he was hidden from the road by bushes and trees, he raised his hand in the air and made a circular motion that meant *assemble on me*.

The men of the second platoon crawled through the woods and formed a circle around him. Their faces were grimy and showed signs of exhaustion. Corporal Banes was chewing a matchstick. Private Nowicki looked at his BAR as though he wanted to dismantle and clean it. Albright was picking his nose.

Mazursky cleared his throat and spat a lunger onto the snow at his feet. He was on his knees, as were the others in the platoon. Their rifle butts were buried in the snow and their barrels pointed in the air.

"The road's just ahead," Mazursky said. "We're gonna have to cross it fast. I didn't see anybody when I just went to take a look, but that don't mean nobody's out there. We're gonna cross all at once in one mad rush. I'll go out first to make sure the coast is clear. You'll all be at the edge of the woods over there and you'll all be able to see me. When I give the double-time signal, run like a bastard across the road and don't stop until you've found some natural cover. I don't know what's on the other side of the road, but there's got to be something there. Probably trees just like over here. Once you land, stay still and await further orders from me. Any questions?"

Corporal Banes raised his hand. "Maybe it'd be better if we went over one squad at a time."

"I think it'd be faster if we all went over at once."

"But we're liable to attract more attention that way."

"If anybody's looking, they'll see us whether it's one squad or one platoon. So it's best to just get the fuck over there. Any more questions?"

Nobody said anything.

"Okay, let's form up squad by squad at the edge of the woods. Move out."

The soldiers crawled to the edge of the woods and stopped, peering up at the Dillendorf road. Mazursky and Albright moved behind them and stopped twenty yards back. Mazursky and Albright moved behind them and stopped twenty yards back. Mazursky looked at the men and thought they were too bunched together. He gave the signal to Banes to spread them out. Otherwise one mortar shell would wipe out half of them.

Banes crawled up and down the line and moved the men apart. Now they were a long khaki line at the base of the trees. It was now or never.

Mazursky looked at Albright. "I'm going alone again. You take a position on the line. When I give the signal, go over the road with everybody else, and then look for me."

"Right, Sarge."

"Let's go."

They crawled toward the line. When they reached it they stopped. Mazursky looked to his right and left. The coast was still clear. He crawled forward, out of the protection of the trees. Every man in the platoon watched him climb down the gully and up the other side.

Mazursky kept looking to his right and left. His mouth was dry and he expected a shot to go right through his gizzard at any moment. He felt vulnerable as a turtle lying on its back. Raising his eyes to the level of the road, he breathed a sigh of relief when he saw that it was still clear. There was no point in wasting any time. He raised his arm and pumped it up and down. Then he got up and ran across the road as he heard the second platoon come out of the woods behind him. He went down the gully on the other side and ahead were some woods. He tripped and fell, got up, and ran into the woods. Stopping, he dropped to his knees and looked behind him.

The second platoon, their rifles at high port arms, came charging across the road. Their helmets bounced around on their heads and their canteens flapped on their hips. They came down the gully and ran toward the woods. They came fast and didn't look around or fuck around. Soon as they hit the woods they started diving for cover. Suddenly the woods were still. They had done it. Mazursky was proud of them.

Towering behind the trees was the craggy ridge where the second platoon was to make its stand. It was gray and evil looking, and Mazursky wondered if he was staring at his grave. Something rustled beside him. It was the dog.

"Where the fuck have you been?" Mazursky asked, petting it.

The dog licked his hand.

Chapter Three

THE SECOND PLATOON passed through the small wooded area, crossed a frozen swamp, and climbed the hill to the rocky ridge. The hill was steep, covered with ice and snow, and would be hard for German soldiers to take with the second platoon shooting at them and lobbing down hand grenades. Mazursky was glad that headquarters had at least designated a strong defensive position for them. He was first man on the ridge, and took a quick reconnoiter. There were boulders, ledges, and caves for cover. The sides of the hill were too steep to climb, and Mazursky didn't think the Germans or anybody else could ever get to the summit, which was about fifty yards higher than the ridge.

Corporal Banes walked up to Mazursky. Banes' helmet was on the back of his head and his eyes were glassy with fatigue.

"The men are awfully hungry, sergeant," he said.

"They'll eat after we get dug in."

"Jeez!"

"What's the matter."

57

"Half of them can barely stand up."

"Are you talking about them or you?"

"Me too, I guess."

"The sooner we get set up here, the sooner we eat. German bullets are worse than hunger pains."

There were three caves along the ridge. Mazursky positioned the two anti-tank crews in two of them, and two bazooka crews in the third. He deployed a few riflemen in each cave, and the rest of them in a skirmish line along the ledge. Two .30 caliber machine guns would cover the flanks, and the BAR men were spaced evenly among the riflemen on the ledge. He made sure everyone had an equal amount of hand grenades and ammunition. Then he called a meeting in the cave where the first anti-tank squad was, because that was the largest cave.

The men sat around him on the cold stone floor. The walls of the cave were covered with hoarfrost. The men hoped the meeting would be over fast so they could eat. Mazursky looked at his watch; it was 0830 hours. In the distance, from all directions, he could hear the sound of artillery bombardment and small arms fire. Smoke filled the sky and merged with the thick layer of clouds that kept the Air Corps out of action.

Mazursky stood with his back to the wall and looked down at his men. "Okay, this is the poop," he said. "A panzer division is going to be coming down that road in a little while, and we've got to stop it. It shouldn't be too hard. All we have to do is knock out the lead tanks, and that will clog the road. The other tanks won't be able to get through, and if we keep up our fire, they won't be able to drag the ruined tanks out of the way. Anyway, we've got to stop those tanks, because if they get through, they'll chew up the regiment, which is in retreat right now. We've got to hold the tanks until noon, because then the regiment will be in a better defensive position, and reinforcements will be sent up from other sectors. If we don't stop the tanks, the regiment will be wiped out. Any questions?"

Corporal Banes raised his hand. "What happens to us after noontime?"

Mazursky shrugged. "I guess we try to hold on until the Germans are pushed back. Then we can rejoin our company."

"But that might not be for days."

"Any other questions?"

Private Winfield raised his hand. "Did you say that we gotta stop a whole panzer division?"

"That's what I said."

"Do you realize how many tanks are in a panzer division?"

"All we have to do is stop the first three or four, and that'll clog the road."

"How about the troops that come with a panzer division?"

"They won't be able to penetrate this position. We'll all be behind a solid wall of rock. They'll have to climb the hill, and we'll just lob our hand grenades down on them."

Corporal Ginsburg raised his hand. "What happens when we run out of hand grenades?"

Mazursky scratched his nose and looked away. "We got plenty of hand grenades."

"But we'll run out of them sooner or later. And ammo too."

"We'll be okay," Mazursky said, hoping he sounded reassuring.

"For how long?"

"Okay, chow time," Mazursky said, clapping his hands. "I don't want any fires. Eat the shit cold and keep your eyes open, got it? If we spot any German troops we lie down and let them pass. It's the tanks we're worried about, understand? Now go chow down, and don't eat so much that you get sick. I want every squad to post a lookout."

The men returned to their positions, took off their packs, removed cans of C-rations, opened them, and greedily spooned the contents into their mouths. In different circumstances they would have complained about the C-rations, and maybe said C-rations weren't fit for dogs, but now they were hungry and the C-rations tasted great.

Mazursky ate in the first anti-tank squad cave, throwing scraps to the dog. Albright sat opposite him, eating lackadaisically. Albright's helmet lay on the floor of the cave and his pale blonde hair was tousled all over his head. He was nineteen years old.

Mazursky looked at him. "Lose your appetite?"

"I think so."

"I thought you were so hungry before. What happened?"

"Your little speech killed my appetite. I don't think we're gonna get out of here alive."

"I don't give a fuck what you think. Keep your mouth shut."

60

"Why did they have to pick us? Why couldn't they pick some other platoon?"

"I said keep your fucking mouth shut. I'm not going to tell you again. If you can't say something nice, don't say nothing at all."

"I can't think of anything nice to say."

"Then keep your fucking mouth shut."

Mazursky finished his can of franks and beans and then opened a can of fruit cocktail. He really loved fruit cocktail, but could never get enough of it. He'd sworn many times that if he ever got out of the war alive he'd buy a whole crate of fruit cocktail and sit down and eat it all.

But something told him he wasn't going to get out of the war alive.

He looked at Albright over a spoonful of fruit cocktail. "You know what your problem is, Fuckbright?"

"Huh?" Albright thought Mazursky didn't want to speak to him anymore.

"I said you know what your problem is?"

"No."

"Your problem is that you ain't mean. You don't hate. All you want to do is weasel your way out of things, and one of these days somebody is going to step on you. You've got to hate those Germans, Albright. You've got to want to split their skulls and drink their blood. You've got to want to cut out their intestines and chew on them. And gouge out their eyeballs. And stomp on their balls. If you can get yourself in that frame of mind, boy, then maybe you'll be a soldier."

"I hate the Germans, Mazursky. I really do."

"Bullshit, and who are you calling *Mazursky?*"

"I mean, *Sergeant* Mazursky."

"That's better. You don't hate them because you're too worried about saving your own little weasly ass. When you stop worrying so much about yourself, then you'll be able to hate."

Albright looked at Mazursky and went beet red. "Are you trying to say that I'm a coward?"

"Are you trying to say that I'm a coward *what?*"

Albright's eyes flashed with anger "Are you trying to say that I'm a coward, and never mind that sergeant bullshit."

"Sergeant bullshit?"

"That's right." Albright stood up, a wiry little man with bandy legs. "If you're trying to say that I'm a coward, you'll have to kick my ass."

Mazursky looked up at him. He was getting cross because he wasn't finished with his fruit cocktail yet. "That wouldn't be much of a problem."

Steam seemed to be coming out of Albright's ears. "I'm sick of you insulting me and putting me down! You ugly fucking gorilla, I hate your guts!"

Mazursky raised his eyebrows. "Have you gone crazy, Fuckbright? Don't you know that you can be shot for talking to your platoon sergeant that way?"

"We're all gonna get shot anyway when the panzer division comes up the road! This is a suicide mission and everybody knows it! You can kiss my royal ass, Mazursky! Fuck you! Eat shit!" Albright charged forward and kicked the half-full can of fruit cocktail out of Mazursky's hands.

Mazursky looked down in disbelief at his empty hands. Then he looked at the can of fruit cocktail lying on its side on the floor of the cave, its contents spilled out. Last of all he looked at Albright. "Now you've gone too far, you little fuck!"

Albright was bouncing around on the balls of his feet and waving his fists around in the air. "Get on your feet, Mazursky! I'm going to kick your big fat ass all over this cave!"

Mazursky got up and spit in the palms of his hands. "You are, huh?"

"That's right!"

Albright charged Mazursky, flailing at him with both fists. Mazursky merely took a step back, measured his shot, and brought his fist down on the top of Albright's head. Albright slumped to the floor. Mazursky looked down at him, grinning like an ape.

"I'm just liable to turn this little fucker into a soldier some day," he said. "But meanwhile, he owes me a can of fruit cocktail, right?" He looked at the other men in the cave.

"Sure, Sarge," said Private Fischer of the anti-tank crew.

"I'm glad you agree."

Mazursky went to Albright's pack, opened it, found a can of fruit cocktail, and took it out. Sitting, he opened the can with his pocket can opener and drank the contents without benefit of utensils.

Sergeant Mazursky would do just about anything to get an extra can of fruit cocktail.

In the cave where the second anti-tank crew had established their position, Corporal Banes was lunching with Private Robinson of New York City. Robinson, a graduate of Columbia University and the son of a rich stockbroker, had dropped out of Officers Candidate School because he couldn't put up with the happy horseshit, and now was an ordinary rifleman. He was a rather elegant young man with good manners that were slowly deteriorating. He tended to shave more than the others. He had a thin aquiline nose, high cheekbones, and a supercilious mouth.

"This food tastes ghastly," he said, grimacing as he ate.

"If you don't like it, give it to me," said Banes, who liked to associate with Robinson because he thought Robinson had class and some might rub off on him.

"What are you eating?"

"Sausage patties."

"Good grief. Sausage patties. I bet they're made out of horsemeat."

"Horsemeat is much better than sausage patties, take my word for it."

"You've eaten horsemeat?"

"Sure. Back where I come from we eat horsemeat all the time. It's as good as beefsteak."

Robinson shook his head. "Oh Banes, you're such a fucking hillbilly." Like many New Yorkers, Robinson thought that anybody who didn't live in the Big Apple was a hillbilly.

Banes was from Lubbock, Texas, and had never seen a hillbilly before he enlisted in the Army. "I ain't no fucking hillbilly."

"Of course you are."

"Robinson, you wouldn't know a bull's ass from a banjo, you know that? There's a difference between a cowboy, which is what I was, and a hillbilly, which is something that lives in certain southern states and don't generally wear shoes."

"Did you carry a six-gun?"

"Naw, for chrissakes. Texas ain't like you see it in the movies. But I used to carry a rifle in my scabbard whenever I was out on my horse. Use to get a lot of varmints that way."

"Oh, I'm sure you did."

"Are you trying to say that you don't believe me?"

"Of course I believe you," Robinson said, looking down his exquisite nose at Banes. "You couldn't tell a decent lie if your life depended on it."

"Now what in hell's that supposed to mean? You know, Robinson, sometimes I cain't figger out what you're talking about."

"That's because you're a hillbilly."

"I ain't no hillbilly!"

"After this war's over I want you to come to New York with me, Banes. You can stay with me and my family and I'll show you the city. It'll frazzle your so-called mind. I'll take you up to the top of the Empire State Building and you won't believe what you'll see. And I know some girls who'd be just absolutely crazy about you."

Banes looked up from his cold franks and beans. "Really?"

"Sure."

"What part of New York do you live in?"

"Manhattan, of course."

"That a nice place?"

"Part of it is."

"You must live in a good part, huh Robinson?"

"I live on Park Avenue," Robinson said drily.

"It nice there?"

"Very nice."

"Since they call it Park Avenue, there must be a park nearby, right?" Banes smiled broadly at his clever conclusion.

"Wrong."

Banes was crestfallen. "It ain't next to no park?"

"No, it isn't."

"Then how come they call it Park Avenue?"

"I don't know. For the same reason they call Germany Germany, even though there aren't any germs there."

"Oh yes there are germs in Germany. There's germs everywheres."

"But that's not why they call it Germany."

"How do you know?"

"I know."

"Prove it."

"I can't prove it."

Banes looked triumphant. "Then keep your fucking mouth shut about things you don't know anything about." He was overjoyed to have beaten a college graduate in argument.

Robinson speared a piece of frankfurter with his fork. Sometimes he wished he didn't drop out of Officers Candidate School.

Down on the ridge, Private Nowicki, the BAR man,

was re-reading the letter from his girlfriend Shirley, as he ate a can of cold corned beef hash. He still couldn't get it through his head that she had fallen in love with a 4-F welder who earned a hundred dollars a week after she had let him, Nowicki, kiss her bare nipples and stick his fingers into her coozie.

Seated next to Nowicki was Private Deesing from San Francisco. A broad-shouldered broad-hipped man with thick thighs, a blond mustache, and eyes that looked enormous behind his glasses, Deesing had been a white-collar worker before getting drafted. He was eating a cold can of meatballs, as he watched Nowicki reading the letter.

"Get another letter from your girlfriend?" Deesing asked. He was an affable guy who liked to engage in conversation with his fellow man.

"No."

"Oh, your mother wrote?"

"My mother don't know how to write."

"Then who's the letter from?"

"Shirley."

"Isn't that your girl friend?"

"Yes."

"I thought you said you didn't get another letter from her."

"I didn't," Nowicki said sadly.

"You mean you're still reading the same old fucking letter?"

"Yes."

"Gee, you must really be in love with her."

"I really m."

"You poor son of a bitch."

"You can say that again."

"She's in love with some 4-F?"

"Yes. He's a welder and he makes a hundred dollars a week."

"And you're still in love with her anyway?"

"Yup."

"She must be some babe."

"Oh, she is," Nowicki replied, chewing a mouthful of beans. "Pretty as an angel."

"She must be a real hot piece of ass too."

Nowicki nearly choked on his beans. "Don't talk about Shirley that way!"

"You mean she isn't a real hot piece of ass?"

"Well, I don't know."

"You never plunked her?"

Nowicki shook his head in embarrassment. "No."

"How come?"

"She wouldn't let me."

"None of them let you, stupid. You have to make them."

"Oh, I couldn't make Shirley do a thing like that before we were married."

"That was your mistake. If you'd plunked her good, she would never have run off."

"But she kept saying no."

"When women say no, they mean yes. They don't even realize this themselves, but it's true." Deesing considered himself a great expert on women and love. "You just should have taken off her pants and stuck it in."

Nowicki shook his head. "Shirley's a nice girl. You don't do things like that to nice girls."

"Who doesn't? I do all the time. And they love it. Nice girls like it more than anybody else. And they're more depraved than other girls, once you reach them. You should have chained her to the radiator and fucked her brains out."

"Chained her to the radiator!"

"She would have loved it. She'd be praying for your safe return right now if you had. And you should have eaten her, too."

"What do you mean, eaten her?"

"I mean putting your face between her legs and chewing on her snatcherino."

Nowicki stuck his tongue out. "What!"

"You haven't done that?"

"No!"

"I hate to say it, Nowicki, but that was your big mistake. Girls love to get eaten. When you didn't plunk her or eat her she probably figured you were no fun and started thinking about finding someone else."

Nowicki had been torturing himself over the loss of Shirley for the past month, but this was a new angle on the problem. "You think that's what did it?"

"No question about it," Deesing said definitively.

"What does it taste like?"

"Just like ham and eggs."

"But isn't it dirty down there?"

"No dirtier than that corned beef hash you're eating. And it tastes a whole lot better, believe me."

"Are you sure you're not shitting me, Deesing?"

"Of course I'm not shitting you. I mean, you're the BAR man around here. My life depends on you, so I wouldn't shit you. Not ever. I'll tell you what to do with Shirley. When you get home, go to a store and buy some black lace ladies underwear and some black mesh ladies stockings. Then go see Shirley and ask her to put them on. Next you tie her to the bed and start plunking her. After you finish plunking her you should eat her. Then make her eat you. Then roll her over onto her stomach and put it up her dirt road. After that, I guarantee it, she'll be in love with you for the rest of your life."

Nowicki shook his head. "Gee, I don't know, Deesing."

"I know. Do what I say and you'll be all right. None of my girl friends ever wrote me and said she had fallen in love with a 4-F welder. And I get letters every mail call from girls. I don't even have time to answer them, and they keep writing me anyway. Listen to me. I know what I'm talking about. Next time you get the chance, write her a letter and tell her that you don't care how many boyfriends she's got, and when you get home you're going to do all the things to her that you should have done before you left for the Army. Describe all the details. I guarantee that she'll start writing nice letters to you again."

"Gee, I don't know, Deesing."

"What have you got to lose?"

"Nothing, I guess."

"Then do it, first chance you get. Okay, buddy?"

"I guess so," Nowicki said weakly.

DOOM PLATOON

Pfc. MacDoodle sat behind a boulder on the ridge and sharpened his bayonet on a special Arkansas Washita stone he'd bought at a hardware store before embarking for Europe. MacDoodle hailed from Chicago and had been in trouble with the police since early youth. He'd already spend a few years in the can for beating up on people, and when he got arrested again the judge gave him the choice of either joining the Army or going back to jail. MacDoodle joined the Army.

He was a thickset redheaded Irishman and right now he had doubts about his choice. If he'd gone to jail he'd get out in a few years, but it didn't look like he was going to get out of the Army alive. He figured that very night he'd be food for the buzzards. The second platoon might have a lot of tough guys, but they weren't tougher than a panzer division. Well, if he was going to die, he'd take a lot of krauts with .him.

Private Winfield sat down next to MacDoodle. "Can I borrow the stone when you're finished?"

"Sure, if you let me use your file."

"I was going to use it right now. Maybe when I'm finished with it you'll be finished with your stone and we can swap."

"Good idea. You're always thinking, Winfield."

Winfield was a big rawboned farm boy from Iowa. He spread his poncho on the ground and then emptied bullets from his clips onto it. Taking out his little file, he grated down the points of the bullets, putting an X across them. That way if the bullet hit a German, it'd do more damage. For instance, if you hit a German in the arm with an ordinary bullet, it might just pass through leaving behind a superficial wound. If you hit him in the arm with a filed bullet, which were known as dum-dums, you'd take his whole fucking arm off. Dum-dums were outlawed by the Geneva Convention, but Winfield didn't give a fuck about that.

"You hear about what happened between Mazursky and Albright?" Winfield asked, filing down a bullet.

"No."

"Mazursky just beat up Albright and stole some of his food."

"Oh that Mazursky's sure a pisser. He's the meanest man I ever met, and I've met some mean ones. In civilian life they put guys like that in jail or in looney bins."

"Mazursky couldn't make it in civilian life. He's just a fucking killer."

"So in civilian life he could be a gangster. He'd be a very good gangster. His blood's colder than that piece of ice sitting over there. I met some gangsters in my life and I know what I'm talking about."

"You have?" Winfield asked. Winfield was a little in awe of MacDoodle, because MacDoodle was from Chicago.

"Sure. I even saw Al Capone once."

"You did?"

"Sure. He used to come into my neighborhood all the time. Lots of Italians lived in my neighborhood. They used to make whisky in their bathtubs during the Prohibition and Capone used to buy it from them."

"How do you think Mazursky would stack up to Capone."

"On a straight man to man basis, Mazursky would

chew up Capone and spit out the pieces."

"No shit?"

"Listen," MacDoodle said in a knowing way. "You just joined this company before we left for Europe, but I was with this company for a year of training at Fort Benning. I know Mazursky a lot better than you do. I remember one night some of us were in a bar in some shit-kicking little town, don't remember the name right now. Anyway, Mazursky got into a beef with some paratrooper and hit him over the head with a bottle of whisky. The bottle broke and then Mazursky took the jagged edge and twisted it into the poor bastard's face. It was awful. I mean, I been in some gory situations in my day, but it was one of the most worst things I've ever seen. Mazursky almost killed the guy. In fact, he might've killed him for all I know. I never saw the guy again."

"What he do that made Mazursky so mad?"

"Nothing."

"Nothing? He almost killed him for nothing?"

"Mazursky don't like paratroopers."

"You mean he did it just because the other guy was a paratrooper?"

"That's right. Whatever you do, don't ever say the word *paratrooper* in front of Mazursky. It makes him go crazy."

"How come?"

"I heard it has something to do with a woman. Mazursky was married once, and his wife left him for a paratrooper. He beat the fuck out of the guy, and was busted down to private. And he'd been the first sergeant of a company at the time."

"No shit?"

"No shit. So don't ever say nothing about paratroopers around him."

"Are you kidding? I'm not that crazy."

"You know, I feel sorry for any German who goes up against Mazursky. Them Germans are civilized people, you know. They got culture. But Mazursky is just basically a sadist. All he wants to do is fuck over people. He' s a killer. He loves the sight of blood."

"I'm glad he's on our side and not theirs."

"Me too."

Farther down the skirmish line, Private Braithwaite of Detroit was enjoying an after dinner smoke with Private Hartman of Dillwyn, a small town in the great state of Kansas. They didn't know each other very well but had been deployed next to each other and thought they might as well talk.

Hartman had big ears, a big nose, and big teeth. His nickname was Jayhawker, which was what people from Kansas were sometimes called. "You know what I'm gonna do after the war, Braithwaite?" he asked dreamily, trying not to dwell on the fact that the odds were against his surviving the day, never mind the war.

"What?" asked Braithwaite, who also was anxious not to think about depressing things.

"I'm gonna get me about five hundred acres of good bottom land and raise me some corn."

"What the hell is bottom land?" interrupted Braithwaite.

Hartman squinted his eyes at Braithwaite. "You don't know what bottom land is?"

"I wouldn't have asked you if I knew what it was."

"Damn, I can't imagine a grown man not knowing what bottom land is."

"Well what the fuck is it?"

"Bottom land is the land around water. It's very good land for growing things."

"Oh, I get it."

"And anyways, I'm gonna have some pigs too. I'll feed the corn to the pigs, and then sell the pigs to the meat company. And I'll put the pig shit back into the bottomland. Nothing will get wasted, you see. There's money in raising pigs, you know. What do you think those sausage patties are made out of?"

"Pig shit."

"That's what they taste like, but that ain't what they're made out of. They're made out of pig meat."

"You could fool me."

"Oh, they weren't that bad."

"Oh yes they were."

"Oh no they weren't. And I'll have me a nice little garden where I'll raise corn and strawberries for my own use, and a chicken coop for fresh eggs. The good thing about farming, you see, is that you'll never have to worry about going without food."

Braithwaite looked him in the eye. "You ever fuck a pig, Jayhawker?"

"Fuck a pig!"

"Sure, fuck a pig. You farm boys are fucking animals all the time, aren't you?"

"Hell, no!"

LEN LEVINSON

"That's what I heard."

"Well, not all the time," Hartman said indignantly.

"What's pig pussy like?"

"I ain't never screwed no pig."

"How about a sheep? I hear they're just like women."

"We ain't got no sheep around where I live."

"Cows?"

"Yeah, I done it to a couple of cows in my day."

"What's it like."

"Well, you got to be careful you don't fall off the stool. You see, you gotta stand on a stool if you wanna do it to a cow. My favorite screwing, outside of women of course, is chickens. You ain't lived until you screwed a chicken."

Braithwaite looked at him blankly. "A chicken?"

"Yeah, a chicken."

"You've done it to chickens?"

"Ain't nothing like chicken pussy."

"No shit?"

"I wouldn't lie to you."

"Chicken pussy?"

"That's right. After this war's over, you come down to Dillyn to see me, hear? I'll take you out to the chicken coop and show you a real good time."

"Okay," Braithwaite said weakly, wondering if he was dreaming.

"Hey, what are you going to do after the war, Braithwaite?"

"Who, me?"

"I don't mean your brother."

"I'm going into the banking business," Braithwaite said. "That's where the big money is."

DOOM PLATOON

"Your family own a bank or something like that?"

"No, but when I get out of the Army I'm going to get a job in a bank and work my way up to the top. You said before that the good thing about farming is that a farmer never has to worry about going without food. That's not always so, because sometimes farmers have bad years and the banks have to foreclose. But nobody ever forecloses on banks, because banks own everything. You see, farmers think they own their land, but they seldom do own it free and clear. Usually they have to take a loan from the bank to buy the land, so the bank really owns it. In the same way, the banks own just about everything else in this country, like houses, stores, even factories. Banks are always collecting money from everybody. When times are bad and people can't pay the banks, then the banks just take all the houses, farms, and factories. They wait until times are good and then sell them for more money. So you see, if you got to work for a living, it doesn't make sense to work for anybody else except a bank."

Hartman shook his head. "Well, I don't know. I'd rather be out working in the fresh air."

"I'd rather be where the money is," Braithwaite replied.

At the right flank of the ridge, Private Johnson of Baton Rouge, Louisiana was on sentry duty. He'd had to eat standing up and watching the road. It occurred to him that he always seemed to pull more guard duty and more K.P. than anybody else. A pug nosed young man with a shock of unmanageable flaxen hair, he'd regretted enlisting in the Army since his very first morning at Fort Sill, Oklahoma. The Army wasn't fun, as he'd thought it would be. It was hard work, not enough sleep, lousy food, sadistic sergeants, and bullets flying at you all the time.

While thinking of how much he hated the Army, he noticed that in the distance the road had somehow gotten shorter. Before it was shining with ice and snow, but now it was dark. He squinted his eyes and bent forward over the boulder. The road had become dark because there were vehicles on it, he realized. And those vehicles were coming from the direction of the enemy lines. It was the panzer division.

Turning, Johnson climbed ten feet up the rocky ledge to the cave where Mazursky was leaning back, smoking his next-to-last cigar near the anti-tank squad. Albright was a few feet away, cleaning his M-1. The dog lay sleeping at Mazursky's big feet.

Johnson burst into the cave. 'Sergeant Mazursky—they're coming!"

Mazursky grabbed the binoculars lying beside him, jumped up, and ran to the opening of the cave. Bracing his shoulder against the wall, he peered through the binoculars. Sure enough, down the road he saw the panzer division coming. In front were two tanks with their tops open and their tank commanders standing there, looking around. Mazursky could make out their black berets and their radio headsets. He lowered the binoculars and turned around.

"Here they come," he said. "Let's get ready for them."

Then he glanced at his watch. It was 1000 hours.

Chapter Four

THE SECOND PLATOON got set to attack the panzer column. Mazursky inspected his position, making sure his men were where they should be, and telling them the plan of attack. There was a large spruce tree at the side of the road about a hundred yards before them. When the lead tanks came abreast of that tree, the second platoon was to open up with all they had. The first anti-tank crew under Mazursky would try to hit the tank on the right. The second anti-tank squad under Corporal Banes would try to take out the one on the left. The various bazooka men would aim for tanks directly behind the front two. The soldiers with small arms weapons were to keep the enemy soldiers pinned down and to repulse any assault. They had to hold out until noon. Somehow.

Mazursky entered the cave of the second anti-tank squad and inspected the gun on its tripod. He looked through its sight and the cross hairs were on that part of the road opposite the spruce tree.

"Keep firing until you hit the fucking tank," he said, "and once you hit it, hit it again. When you're sure it's out of action, aim for a tank farther down the line. Got it?"

"Yes sergeant."

Mazursky went down on the ridge and worked out a firing plan so that the BAR men would have overlapping fields of fire. "When the troops attack, they're going to come through the woods in front of us. You won't be able to hit them there, but once they come out into the open on that swamp down there, rip the bastards apart. Understand?"

"Yes sergeant."

"FIX BAYONETS!"

They hooked the bayonets on their rifles as Mazursky climbed up to the cave where the first anti-tank crew was. At the mouth of the cave, he ducked down behind the boulders and took out his binoculars. Peering through them, he saw the panzer column coming about a half-mile off. Eight tanks were in front, and behind them were four personnel carriers with mounted machine guns. Then there were more tanks and more personnel carriers all the way back to the horizon. Mazursky gulped. There were light artillery pieces behind each personnel carrier. They'd use that artillery to slowly blast the hill away until the second platoon, like a colony of ants, were exposed. Then the massacre would begin.

The anti-tank crew was pale and steely-eyed behind their gun.

"Everything okay boys?" Mazursky asked.

"Yes sergeant."

"Make the first shot count. You might not get a second one."

"Right sergeant."

In the cave with the second anti-tank crew, Private Robinson, the New Yorker who'd flunked out of Officers Candidate School, was stacking clips of ammunition beside his position. He was lying on the ground and his M-1 stuck out between two large boulders. It'd be hard for somebody to shoot him; the only way they'd get him would be to lob an artillery shell into the cave, but its mouth was small and they'd made it smaller by piling up boulders. He was a crack shot with an M-1, and at a range of two hundred yards, he knew he'd have no trouble killing Germans. But he knew that sooner or later the Germans would swarm over the position, and then it'd be bayonets hand to hand. He didn't like the idea of that, because he wasn't particularly strong, and he knew that in hand-to-hand combat, the strongest man would probably win. The thought of a cold German bayonet slicing through his guts made him break out in a cold sweat. He hoped that when the end came, he'd be lucky enough to get a bullet through his brain.

Down on the ridge, Private Nowicki was looking through his BAR sights at the oncoming panzer columns. He'd been in front line combat long enough to know that the second platoon didn't have a chance, and particularly not the BAR men, because automatic weapons like the BAR tended to attract hand grenades and all manner of rifle and machine gun fire. He turned to Deesing, who was lying beside him, nervously pushing the safety in and out of the trigger guard of his M-1.

"Hey Deesing," Nowicki said.

"What?"

"Listen. I want you to do me a favor."

"Now?"

"Yeah."

"What the fuck is it?" Deesing looked at him, his full lips sticking out petulantly. He was not in a particularly good mood.

"First I want you to promise me that you'll do it."

"How the fuck can I promise to do it if I don't know what it is?"

"You can do it. It won't be hard. It's just a little favor. C'mon, promise."

"Oh fuck, okay. I promise."

"You sure?"

"Yes I'm sure."

"If I die, I want you to go to my home town and say goodbye to Shirley for me."

"What if I die too?"

"You're not going to die."

"Why not?"

"Guys like you never die. You got Lady Luck on your side."

"What makes you think so?"

"Because you always win at craps."

"I don't know if I can beat a bullet."

"You will. Will you go say goodbye to Shirley for me?"

Deesing was sure he'd get killed too, but it wouldn't cost him anything to give Nowicki some piece of mind. "Sure, I'll say goodbye to her for you."

"You promise."

"Yeah, I promise."

Nowicki smiled. "Thanks a lot, Deesing."

"There's just one problem," Deesing said.

"What's that?"

"I don't know where she lives."

"Oh, that's right too. I'll write down her address." Nowicki took out the little notebook and pen he carried, and a photograph of Shirley fell out. "This is a picture of her," he said, picking it up. "Take a look." He handed the picture to Deesing then wrote down the address.

Lying on his stomach, Deesing looked at the picture of Shirley. It was a formal portrait done by a professional photographer in a studio. Shirley had blonde hair, large eyes, an oval face, and the kind of mouth born to give blowjobs. "This is Shirley?" Deesing asked, wide-eyed. He'd always thought she was some ugly little broad.

"Yeah, that's Shirley. What do you think of her?"

"She's okay."

"I guess she's not your type. She's just a small town girl."

"Yeah." Deesing handed back the picture, and accepted Shirley's address. Folding it carefully, he put it in his wallet. He didn't know how, but somehow he was going to survive the war and then go to Pittsburgh and see Shirley whether Nowicki died or not. He'd tie the little bitch to a bed and screw her till she fainted. Then he'd throw a bucket of water on her and screw her again.

Nowicki didn't realize it, but he'd given Deesing a reason to live.

On the road, the panzer division advanced steadily.

Mazursky followed it with his binoculars and could make out the features of the men standing up in the lead tanks. The one on the left was an officer, and the one on the right a non-com. They both were about twenty years old and very clean-cut looking. Mazursky didn't like people who were clean-cut looking because they got all the advantages in life while ugly brutes like himself got all the shit. Mazursky put down the binoculars to rest his eyes, and looked at Albright, who was lying a few feet away, sighting down the barrel of his M-1. Mazursky smiled. Albright sure didn't look clean-cut. He looked like a little fucking rat who'd steal your wallet if you weren't looking.

"How you doing, Fuckbright?" Mazursky asked.

Albright didn't look at him. "Don't worry about me," he said bitterly.

"I didn't say I was worried about you, Fuckbright. I was just asking how you were. And you'd better answer me or I'll kick your teeth in."

"I'm okay."

"Good."

Mazursky brought the binoculars to his eyes and looked at the panzers. They had rounded the last bend before the fatal spruce tree marker. He didn't need his binoculars anymore. He looked at the three men from the weapons platoon who were surrounding the anti-tank gun.

"You guys ready?" Mazursky asked.

Corporal Winograd from Providence, Rhode Island looked through the sights. "I've got the bastards dead on." His finger tightened around the sights.

"Make the first shot count."

DOOM PLATOON

"I'll get him," Winograd said cockily. In point of fact, Winograd was an expert with an anti-tank gun. An engineering student at Brown University when he'd enlisted, he was mechanically inclined and knew his weapon from every possible point of view. Given a reasonable chance, Winograd could be counted on to hit his target. He'd trained his crew to re-load quickly. Mazursky didn't know it but he had one of the best anti-tank crews in the whole U.S. Army right next to him.

The tanks rumbled inexorably toward the spruce tree marker. Mazursky laid his sights on the young cherubic-looking officer in the lead tank on the left. He'd like to drill him through the head, but he had to wait until the anti-tank guns fired.

Closer and closer and tanks came. The officer and non-coms in the lead tanks looked around at the countryside. They'd been training for weeks for this major counter-offensive that Hitler hoped would change the face of the war. Their plan was to slice through the British and American armies, outflank them, and push them back to Antwerp.

The tanks were only twenty yards from the spruce tree. Every man in the second platoon tensed behind his weapon. The tanks kept coming. The German officer was looking up at the ridge and caves where the second platoon was. On his face there grew an expression of concern. He'd seen something.

"Oh-oh," Mazursky murmured.

The German officer raised his binoculars to his eyes. Corporal Winograd had the tank in the dead center of his sight. The tank came abreast of the spruce trees. The German officer lowered his binoculars abruptly and shouted into his headset. Winograd pulled the trigger of his antitank gun.

It made its muffled *poof* sound and kicked slightly.

On the road, the shell hit the tank where its turret met its body, and exploded. A shell from the other anti-tank gun hit the tank beside it in the treads. The second platoon opened fire with everything they had. The bazookas fired. The BAR men raked the personnel carriers with automatic weapons fire. German soldiers leapt from the personnel carriers and ran into the woods at both side of the road. Smoke filled the air around the tanks.

Mazursky peered through the smoke and his heart was gladdened when he saw the German officer standing in the turret of the tank with his shoulders and head missing. But in the other tanks they were battening down the hatches and swinging their big guns around. The second platoon's anti-tank squads knocked out two more tanks and one personnel carrier. German soldiers were lying dead in the road and the gully. The German panzer column could no longer advance.

But they could fight back.

The cannons and machine guns mounted on the tanks opened fire on the second platoon's position. The first salvo landed just beneath Mazursky's cave, and the whole hill trembled. The second salvo hit the boulder that Winfield and MacDoodle were hiding behind. The sound of the explosion was so loud it disoriented them and made them deaf for a few minutes. Private Johnson on the right flank happened to look up at the wrong time and caught a machine gun burst in the face. His blood and brains splattered the men near him, but they kept firing their weapons.

Mazursky looked at his watch It was 1030 hours. Somehow the second platoon had to hold out for another hour and a half. Shells and bullets rained down on their position, and he didn't see how they could do it. He sighted down his carbine at the road. Germans were abandoning the damaged tanks. One of them was jumping down over the smoking treads. Mazursky shot him in mid-air. When the German landed on the ground he collapsed and never got up again.

Down on the ledge, Nowicki had forgotten all about Shirley and was calmly gunning down fleeing Germans with his BAR. The weapon stopped firing, he ejected the empty clip, pushed in a new one, and resumed firing at the tank crews running for shelter in the woods. A machine gun burst slammed into the rocks in front of him, and he ducked. When it passed he looked up again and noticed German soldiers attacking from out of the wooded area below. He angled his BAR down and opened fire on them. He hit two, but they were pouring out of the woods in droves. Beside him, Deesing removed a hand grenade from one of his lapels, yanked the pin, and hurled it.

The hand grenade fell lazily through the air, resembling a ball that children might play with, and landed in the midst of the Germans. It exploded with a thunderous sound, blowing Germans to bits. The Germans kept coming. Other second platoon men threw hand grenades, which spread bloody devastation among the Germans. But they kept coming.

The machine guns and cannons on the tanks stopped firing as the German soldiers neared the crest of the ridge. Realizing that, the men of the second platoon stood up and threw hand grenades down the hill fast as they could pull the pins. Others fired rifles at the Germans fast as they could pull the trigger. The Germans faltered and began to fall back, but some kept coming. Nowicki stood up with his BAR, and firing from the hip, mowed them down. The lead German, an officer, made it to the ridge and didn't realize he was all alone, and that the others were retreating. He leapt over the barricade and found himself face to face with Private Hartman, the Jayhawker. Before the officer could fire his Luger, Hartman ran him through with his bayonet.

Farther down the line, a German soldier realized, just as he approached the ridge, that his comrades had retreated. He turned to join them, but four hands came over the ridge and grabbed him by the collar and shoulder.

MacDoodle and Winfield dragged the German soldier kicking and screaming behind the ridge. They kicked him in the balls and punched him in the face. MacDoodle took out his Chicago switchblade and cut the German's throat from ear to ear. Blood gushed out of the gash and the German's mouth. In swift strong strokes MacDoodle cut off his ears and his nose. He gouged out the German's eyes. Opening the German's pants, he cut off the German's pecker and stuffed it in the German's mouth. Then he and Winfield threw the German over the edge of the ridge, and the German rolled down the steep hill.

"Them's my boys," Mazursky said proudly from his cave.

DOOM PLATOON

The men of the second platoon cheered wildly at the retreating Germans, but their joy was short lived. The German tanks and machine guns started firing again, pinning down the second platoon once more. The men of the second platoon knew that the German soldiers below were getting ready for another assault.

Private Winfield looked up quickly to see what the German soldiers were doing below. He wanted to grab another one and cut him up. Just then a shell exploded directly in front of him. A piece of shrapnel cut his head in half lengthwise. MacDoodle watched calmly as his buddy was thrown backwards against the hill that led to the caves.

"You shouldn't stick your head up like that," he said to the corpse.

A shell from a German tank landed a miraculous direct hit in the second cave, killing instantly all members of the anti-tank crew, and wounding Corporal Banes. Private Robinson, the New Yorker who'd flunked Officers Candidate School, somehow had not been touched at all.

When the smoke cleared he looked around him at the smoke and carnage. Blood and meat were on the walls, ceiling, and floor. His ears were ringing and when he touched them he had blood on his hands. He realized with horror that something had been ruptured inside his ears.

"Hello," he said aloud, wondering if he were deaf. But he heard himself, and knew he wasn't.

"Medic!" called out Corporal Banes weakly.

Robinson crawled over to him. "We don't have any medics."

Banes had a wild crazy look in his eyes. "Medic!"

Robinson realized Banes was shell-shocked. He looked him over and saw blood pouring from his right hip.

"Just lay still there, Corporal," Robinson said. "I'll fix you right up."

Robinson removed his bayonet from his rifle and cut away Banes' pants. It was a big ugly shrapnel wound; it looked like Banes' hip was crushed. Every soldier carried a wound dressing on his belt, but this wound was too big for that. Robinson opened Banes' pack and took out a tee shirt and a pair of pants. Folding them, he pressed them against the wound. He knew it wouldn't help much, but he had to do something. Banes eyes were closed and he was turning white. He'd gone into shock.

In the other cave, Mazursky peered between the two boulders in front of him at the road. One tank had attempted to go around the destroyed tanks by driving down the gully beside the road, but it went down at an angle and tipped over. Another tank turned around in the road and attempted to go down the gully straight, but in the bottom there wasn't enough room to turn around so it had to go up the other side. That landed it in the woods, where it was trapped by the thick old trees. Mazursky figured that the next step would be to blow the trees out of the way. Sure enough, a group of Germans with explosives came running from back down the column. Mazursky took aim with his carbine and fired at them, but missed. He fired again and brought one down. Albright fired his M-1 and brought another down. On the ridge, one of the BARs opened up on them, and the Germans scattered for cover. But a German mortar round landed next to that BAR man, and after the explosion the BAR man's body parts were all over the hill.

DOOM PLATOON

Winograd calmly took aim through the sight of his anti-tank gun, pulled the trigger, and blew the treads off another tank. His crew re-loaded, he fired again, and demolished the turret of a different tank. The road was becoming a mass of ruined tanks.

Mazursky looked at Winograd and grinned. "You're a good fucking man, you know that?"

Winograd looked through his sight. "Tell me something I don't know." He pulled the trigger and knocked out another tank.

But the tanks and artillery pieces were zeroing in on the embattled second platoon. A shell burst tore a huge hole in the defensive perimeter on the ridge, killing four men. Another blew in the flank, killing Private Levinson.

The German infantry soldiers came out of the woods and charged the hill once more. The men of the second platoon couldn't see them, but when the shelling stopped they knew trouble was on the way. They looked up and saw the Germans scrambling up the hill. The Germans fired their rifles as they came; some of them threw hand grenades. One of the Germans, a burly fellow over six feet tall, threw one with all his might, and it went into the opening of the cave above the ridge.

The hand grenade landed next to Private Albright. Albright was between Mazursky and the hand grenade. On the other side of Mazursky was the anti-tank crew. Albright stared at the hand grenade for an eternity that really lasted only a split second. Then, quick as a fox, he took off his helmet, dropped it over the grenade, and covered the helmet with his body.

The grenade exploded with a deafening roar. Albright went flying into the air, and landed on his back. His stomach was a huge mass of blood and guts. But no one else was hurt in the cave.

Mazursky, his head reverberating from the sound of the explosion, crawled to Albright and bent over him. Albright was still alive, but just barely. He blinked his eyes. Blood foamed out of his mouth.

"How'd...you...like...that...one...Sarge?" Albright asked.

"It was real good, kid. Real good." Mazursky patted him on the head and looked at the gut wound. There was nothing that could be done. Not even if there were four doctors and a hospital room.

"It's...getting...dark...Sarge."

"Well, it's almost night, kid."

"Will...I...be...okay?"

"Sure you will. It's only a little wound."

"I...can't...feel...anything."

"That's because I just gave you a shot of morphine."

"You...ain't...got...no...morph— "

Albright coughed, and a gob of blood came out of his mouth.

"Listen kid, I'm real sorry I hit you today, got me?"

Albright turned his face away and closed his eyes. Mazursky bent over and pressed his ear against Albright's chest. He could hear no heartbeat.

"How is he?" asked Winograd, looking back from his prone position behind the anti-tank gun.

"He's dead," Mazursky said, his eyes closed. "He always was a stupid little fuck. He should have thrown the hand grenade out instead of jumping on it like an asshole. Goddamn Fuckbright. Stupid little bastard." Mazursky made his eyes tighter, but the tears came out anyway.

Below him, the Germans were advancing up the hill before the murderous fire of the second platoon. A German officer shouted orders as he led his troops upwards, a Luger in his right hand. Nowicki took a bead on his chest and pulled the trigger of his BAR. It bucked against his shoulder as it spit out hot lead. The German officer went flying backwards, blood spurting from a hole in his chest.

But the Germans kept coming. They poured out of the woods, crossed the swamp that now was a mass of broken ice, dead bodies, blood, and mud, then charged the hill. The men of the second platoon rolled hand grenades down at them and fired fusillade after fusillade. The Germans kept coming, and there were a great many of them. They came through the grenade blasts and they came through the hail of bullets.

A German tried to climb over the ridge but MacDoodle stood up and hit him in the face with the butt of his rifle. Another German vaulted over the ledge but before he could land, Mac-Doodle ran his bayonet through his guts. A third German made it onto the ridge and charged Private Morelli, who shot wild and missed. The German shot straight and hit Morelli in the chest, and as Morelli slumped to the ground, the German grunted and rammed his bayonet into Morelli's heart. As the German was pulling out his bayonet, he was slammed over the head with an entrenching tool in the hand of Private Deesing.

The German had his helmet on, so was only stunned. Deesing darted to the side and swung at the German's face, but missed, hitting him in the neck instead, and nearly decapitated him. The German fell in a spray of his own blood.

A dozen Germans were on the ridge now, fighting hand-to-hand with the men of the second platoon. Mazursky looked down from his cave at the action, took a quick measure of the situation, and decided that's where he belonged. Throwing off his steel helmet because it slowed him down, chewing the butt of an unlit cigar, he slid down the side of the cliff, carbine in hand, and joined the men fighting on the ridge.

"PUSH THE FUCKERS BACK!" Mazursky yelled. "RIP OUT THEIR FUCKING GUTS!"

Mazursky let go his carbine because it was too light for hand-to-hand combat, and took the M-1 from one of his dead men. Removing the bayonet, he took it by the barrel and began swinging it like a baseball bat, crowning Germans over the head and swatting them across the face, kicking them in the balls, knocking the wind out of them, breaking their spines. He was bellowing like a madman, spittle flying from his lips, his eyes bulging like a madman. German after German fell before the fury of his attack, and meanwhile, the men of the second platoon were rolling hand grenades at Germans coming from the swamp and managing to prevent any more Germans from gaining access to the ridge.

The last three Germans on the ridge fled before the advancing Mazursky and jumped away to the steep slope of the hill, where they went tumbling asshole over teakettle to the swamp. Mazursky ran back to his carbine, put it on automatic, leaned over the ledge, and pulled the trigger. A carbine can spew forth 900 rounds per minute, and Mazursky sprayed the Germans with hot lead. When one clip was empty, he rammed another into the body of the carbine, all the while chewing his cigar. Nowicki and the other BAR men still alive swept back and forth across the Germans, who were falling back. Other soldiers threw hand grenades or pumped off rounds in their M-1s. It was too much for the Germans. They turned and ran.

When the Germans in the tanks saw their infantry retreating, they opened fire again with machine guns and cannon. The second platoon ducked behind their barricades as hell broke loose around them. One shell scored a direct hit in the cave where Winograd's first anti-tank squad was. Mazursky put on the helmet of a dead soldier lying beside him and looked up to the cave where he'd been only minutes before. Smoke was pouring out of it. If he'd stayed there he'd be in that smoke rising up to the thick oatmeal clouds. But he hadn't stayed there. He'd been lucky, and he wondered how long his luck was going to last.

He looked at his watch. It was 1130 hours.

They had a half hour to go. Shells exploded all around him and bullets whizzed over his head. In a half hour he could pull out or surrender. There was no possible way to pull out, so it would have to be a surrender. He wondered what German POW camps were like. Maybe it'd be better to die here, but he didn't have time to make up his mind. There were too many things to do.

Crouching, he moved to the center of the ridge, crawling over dead Germans and his own dead and wounded. "How're you doing?" he asked each of his men.

"I ain't got no more hand grenades," said MacDoodle.

"So what do you want me to do?"

"Just thought I'd tell you."

"Okay, you told me. If you don't have hand grenades, throw stones."

Moving along, talking to each of his men, Mazursky realized the situation was even worse then he'd thought. There were only four hand grenades left, and most of the men were nearly out of ammunition. He knew that with the next German charge, it would be all over. He looked at his watch. It was 1135 hours. Taking a quick peek over the ledge, he saw tanks in the rear trying to push the damaged tanks off the road. He figured in another fifteen or twenty minutes the Germans would clear the road, and what the hell, that was close enough to 1200 hours. The artillery barrage was intense. Machine gun bullets stitched back and forth and up and down. Mazursky made the signal to *assemble on me.*

The remnants of the second platoon gathered around, their faces streaked with dirt, their eyes white and staring, some limping, others bleeding from cuts and gouges. They were Private Nowicki, the BAR man; Private Stein, the former runner for Lieutenant Smith; Private MacDoodle, the homicidal maniac; Private Hartman, who dreamed of a few hundred acres of good bottom land; Private Robinson, the New York playboy who'd come down from the second cave; Private Whitney, a drunkard who mostly kept to himself; Pfc. Ballard, a grizzled old professional like

Mazursky who'd been busted up and down the ranks many times, and Private Deesing, the sex degenerate. These men, and Mazursky, were all that was left of the second platoon, which had numbered 29 men that morning, and which had been 42 when they went into the Hurtgen Forest two weeks ago.

Mazursky motioned for them to come close, so they could hear him above the sound of shell bursts and machine guns. He spoke loud, his spittle flying into their faces, but they didn't seem to care.

"I ain't gonna lie to you," Mazursky said. " We've just about had it. We can't retreat the fuck out of here, and we've just about completed our mission. We got two choices: we can either surrender, or keep on fighting. I'd rather keep on fighting, because I'm afraid the German POW camps might be no better than dying here. But I'll leave it up to you. What do you want to do?"

"I think we should surrender," Robinson said. "In a POW camp we'll have a chance, but here we'll have no chance at all."

Whitney shook his head, and everybody was surprised because he so seldom expressed himself. "I don't wanna be no damn prisoner," he said, his eyes downcast.

"Me neither," added MacDoodle. "Fuck it, let's go out in a blaze of glory."

Stein looked at him. "Blaze of glory? Are you out of your fucking mind?"

MacDoodle rolled up his sleeve and showed a tattoo that said DEATH BEFORE DISHONOR. "I ain't afraid to die," he said.

Stein shook his head. You couldn't reason with maniacs.

"I'll do whatever Sergeant Mazursky does," Hartman said.

"Me too," added Nowicki.

Ballard cleared his throat. "I say fight."

Deesing shrugged. "I don't see where it makes any difference. We're going to get killed no matter what we do."

Mazursky moved his cigar to the other side of his mouth. "Well, I guess we're going to fight it out. Okay, gather up all the ammo and goodies lying around here and let's give the bastards something to remember us by. Hurry, because they'll probably attack again damn soon."

They forged around on the ridge, taking weapons and ammunition and hand grenades from the bodies of the dead. Mazursky found a Luger and two extra clips of ammunition on the body of a German officer, and another Luger on a dead German sergeant. He worked the mechanism on both of them to make they were okay. Then he slid full loaded clips into each of them and jammed them into his cartridge belt. Five German hand grenades were found and Mazursky showed his men how to use them. Then he walked up to Stein.

"C'mere Stein," he said. "I want to talk to you alone."

Stein went with Mazursky to an end of the ridge. He was a small man with soft brown hair and a brown mustache. He reminded Mazursky of a squirrel. They crouched behind a boulder near the dead staring body of Private Johnson.

"You're a Jew, aren't you Stein?"

Stein was taken aback. "Yeah."

"Well let me tell you something. If through some

miracle you don't get killed up here, and get taken prisoner instead, those krauts are going to be awfully hard on you once they find out you're a Jew. I think you should exchange dog tags and I.D. with one of the other guys lying around here dead, like Johnson over there. That might be better for your health."

Stein nodded. "I think you're right, Sarge."

Mazursky slapped him on the shoulder. "Get cracking."

Stein bent over Johnson, unbuttoned Johnson's jacket, and pulled off his dog tags, exchanging them with his own. He tried not to look at Johnson's staring eyes, which scared him. He'd known Johnson quite well; they'd played chess and drunk beer together in the PX at Fort Benning. Rolling Johnson over, he unbuttoned Johnson's back pocket and took out his wallet. Stein had a better wallet, so he just exchanged all his various I.D. cards for all of Johnson's, and put Johnson's wallet back. Johnson had had some money in his wallet and Stein had been tempted to take it, but he didn't. He couldn't bring himself to rob money from the dead. Next he went through Johnson's pockets and found two letters. He took them and exchanged a letter he'd got from his sister. Finally Stein went through his pockets to make sure he had nothing that could possibly identify him as Jewish. They weren't going to put him into any fucking concentration camp if he could help it.

Farther down the line, Nowicki and Deesing crouched behind a boulder. Nowicki was cleaning the chamber of his BAR.

"Hope it doesn't jam," Nowicki said.

"It hasn't jammed yet today."

"But I've done a lot of firing. That hole might be clogged."

"At this point it doesn't matter much, Nowicki."

"What do you mean?"

"You know fucking well what I mean," Deesing said bitterly. He wasn't exactly enchanted about dying.

Next down the line was Private Robinson, sitting with his back against the rock barricade, thinking about the parties he attended on Park Avenue, and the debutantes he used to screw. He spent his summers yachting off Easthampton on Long Island and his winters skiing in the Laurentian Mountains of Canada. He still didn't understand why he'd let himself flunk out of Officers Candidate School in order to join the Infantry. What had he been trying to prove? That he was a man? He shook his head ruefully. Soon he was going to be a corpse.

Beside him, MacDoodle was sharpening his bayonet, his skin tingling with the thought that he was going to die in a bloody all-out hand-to-hand rampage. A few feet away, Private Hartman was trying to come to terms with the fact that he'd probably never see another farm in his life. On the far right, Private Whitney dozed, his mind blank, while Pfc. Ballard, the old professional soldier, chewed a plug of tobacco and actually thought he was going to get through this alive somehow, because he'd been in so many tight spots before, and had come out alive each time.

Mazursky lit his last cigar, closed his eyes, leaned against a boulder, and thought of Sally Mae, the British girl he'd carried on with before leaving for Omaha Beach. Suddenly gunfire and a commotion erupted below. Mazursky leapt to his feet, his mind switching into its combat mode.

"Here they come!" he bellowed. "Let's give them hell!"

He stuck his carbine over the ledge, pointed down, and pulled the trigger. A spray of bullets cut down three German soldiers. He fired again and cut down two more. Stein threw down a German hand grenade, and quickly as he could, a second one. Nowicki blasted away with his BAR and so did Hartman and Ballard. Robinson threw his last hand grenade. So did MacDoodle and Whitney. The Germans advanced through the smoke and fire, realizing there was little opposition left. Nowicki ran out of BAR ammunition and grabbed an M-1. Mazursky's carbine jammed from the heat of too much rapid firing and he threw it to the ground. There were no more hand grenades at all. Ballard's BAR ran out of ammunition. MacDoodle couldn't find any more clips for his M-1. The Germans came up over the ledge and poured into their position.

Mazursky pulled out his two Lugers, pushed off the safeties, and shot a German right in the face. He shot another German in the body, another in the head, another in the gut, but still they kept coming.

Stein spun around and found himself facing a German soldier over six feet tall. Stein was five feet two, and knew that his last card was being played. "BLOOD AND GUTS!" he screamed, just the way they taught him in bayonet training, and lunged at the German, who batted Stein's M-1 out of the way easily, slammed him in the head with his butt plate, and ran him through. The German pulled his bayonet out and ran at Nowicki, while Stein dropped to his knees, clutched his bleeding chest. I didn't even have a chance against him, Stein thought, tears of pain pouring from his eyes, as he fell forward onto his face.

Nowicki fired an M-1 from the hip and caught the German in the throat, but another German standing to the side fired his rifle at Nowicki point blank and hit him in the shoulder. The force of the bullet knocked Nowicki against the barricade, and the German shot him again. The bullet cut through Nowicki's jacket, through the letter from Shirley, and through his brave heart.

Robinson was fighting for his life against two German soldiers, parrying and lunging with bayonets. He managed to stab one in the gut but his bayonet got stuck in there and while he was trying to pull it out the other German slashed down with his rifle and bayonet, cutting open Robinson's jugular vein, and nearly severing his head from his body.

Ballard, the old professional solider, was standing in the middle of a heap of German soldiers, swinging an entrenching tool with his left hand and brandishing a Colt .45 with his right. A German noncom standing a few feet behind him fired point blank and brought him down.

Mazursky looked about him wildly, his back to the wall that led to the caves, firing the Lugers at German soldiers crowding around him, seeing his men falling, and at that point the Lugers ran out of ammunition. He bent over to get the rifle lying in the hands of a dead German, and something smashed him in the head.

Hartman, who wasn't far away, saw Mazursky go down, and became paralyzed by shock of it. In his momentary pause, two Germans ran him through.

Whitney was shot in the head.

DOOM PLATOON

MacDoodle was felled by a burst from a submachine gun.

And then it was Deesing all alone, Deesing at the end of the ridge lunging and firing his rifle, surrounded by Germans. They retreated and he went after them, his mouth filled with the taste of blood, his mind crazed by the fury of battle. One of them came up behind him and whacked him over the head with his rifle butt.

Deesing crumpled to the earth.

It was exactly 1200 hours.

Chapter Five

MAZURSKY OPENED HIS EYES and found himself lying on a cot in a small walled tent. It was dark, the only light coming from a lantern hanging from the center post. Looking to the side, he saw other cots. Opposite him was a German with a rifle sitting in a chair. A few feet away was another German with a rifle sitting in a chair.

Mazursky realized that he was alive and a prisoner of the Germans. He wondered how badly he'd been hurt. He had a terrific headache and felt a little dizzy. Raising his hands to his head, he felt bandages. Running his hands over his body, he could feel nothing else. Evidently he only had a head wound.

The German opposite him stood up. "You are awake?" he asked with a thick German accent.

"Yes."

The German spoke to the other guard, then left the tent. Mazursky lay back and wondered what'd happened to the other guys. At that moment the man on the cot next to him rolled over and faced him. Mazursky looked and saw Deesing with a bandage on his head.

"Hi Sarge," said Deesing weakly.

"Hello fuckhead. How're you feeling?"

"My head hurts."

"So does mine."

"Do you know where we are?"

"No, do you?"

"If I knew I wouldn't have asked you." Mazursky raised himself and looked over Deesing at the other cots. "Anybody else makes it from the second platoon?"

"I don't think so."

"Who're those guys in the other cots."

"I never saw them before in my life."

The German in the other chair stood up. "Stop talking, you two."

Mazursky dropped onto his back again. It looked like he and Deesing were the only survivors of the second platoon. He was glad he wasn't very friendly with any of them, otherwise he'd be broken up right now. Before the Normandy invasion he'd made the mistake of becoming friends with some of his men, and when they died he fell into a deep depression. He couldn't help feeling bad about Ballard, though. Ballard had been an old professional soldier just like himself. It was only a quirk of fate that caused Mazursky to be the buck sergeant and Ballard to be the Pfc. because both of them had been busted many times, and it easily could have turned out the other way around.

The German soldier returned to the tent and stood beside Mazursky. 'Can you stand up?" he asked.

"I don't know."

"Stand up!" the German ordered, brandishing his rifle.

Mazursky threw off the covers and swung his feet around to the floor. He still had his boots on. Sitting, his head spun a bit, then settled down. Slowly he stood, feeling a little weak in the knees. He was wearing his field jacket, and his helmet was gone. It wouldn't fit over his bandaged head anyway. He felt a little floaty, but otherwise all right.

He looked at the German soldier. "Well, I'm up."

"March out of the tent."

Mazursky walked unsteadily to the opening of the tent, bent to pass through, and came up into a cold winter night. He looked at the sky but could see no moon or stars, and from afar he could hear an artillery battle. Around him were tents lined up in ranks, and across the clearing were four larger tents, which he took to be a command post of some type.

The German pointed with his rifle at the four large tents. "Go there."

"Anything you say, champ."

Mazursky trudged across the crusty snow as the German followed him, his rifle pointed at Mazursky's back. He looked toward the sound of the artillery barrage, and saw light flickering on the horizon. That must be the German front lines, and this was somewhere behind the German lines. He wondered how the 25th Regiment was doing. He hoped they'd made it all right and stopped the German advance on Dillendorf.

They approached one of the large tents.

"Go in," the German said.

Mazursky lowered his head and entered the tent. Raising up again, he saw a young German officer sitting behind a desk. The German officer was lean, had black hair, and wore a monocle in his right eye. He had on the green field uniform of the Wehrmacht, and Mazursky was glad it wasn't the black uniform of the SS.

The German officer rose from his seat and smiled. "Ah, Sergeant Mazursky," he said. "Won't you have a seat?" His English had a clipped German accent, and he pointed to a wooden chair beside his desk. A lantern on his desk illuminated the room.

"Sure," said Mazursky, sitting down.

"I'm Lieutenant Kruger," the German officer said. "I'd like to ask you a few questions."

"Shoot," replied Mazursky, and then regretted his choice of words because the German soldier with the rifle was standing a few paces behind him.

Kruger looked puzzled. "What do you mean by *shoot?*" he asked. "Surely you are not asking me to shoot you."

"It's a slang expression. It means go ahead and ask your questions."

"A slang expression?" Kruger bent over a sheet of paper and wrote something. "I am just making a note of that," he said. "I am trying to understand American slang expressions. There are so many of them."

"How about *fuck you?*" Mazursky asked. "You ever hear that one before?"

"As a matter of fact, no. What does it mean?"

"It means, I hope you're feeling okay."

"Indeed? Well let me write that one down too." Kruger wrote it down while Mazursky fought to keep from laughing. Then Kruger looked up at Mazursky, and took a silver cigarette case from a pocket in his tunic. "Cigarette?" he asked, opening the cigarette case and holding it before Mazursky.

"You wouldn't happen to have a cigar on you, would you?"

"I'm afraid not."

"Then I'll have one." Mazursky leaned forward, took a cigarette and put it in his mouth.

Kruger leaned forward and lit it with a cigarette lighter that matched his cigarette case. He was the son of a wealthy industrialist, a graduate of Heidelberg University, an expert horseman, and an expert fencer.

"Thanks," said Mazursky, puffing the strange cigarette.

"You are welcome, sergeant."

Kruger lit a cigarette for himself, then dropped the lighter in his pocket. The men puffed their cigarettes and blew smoke at each other for a few seconds. The guard, who was not a smoker, started coughing.

Kruger leaned toward Mazursky. "You are a very brave man," he said.

"Who me?"

"Yes. I understand you fought magnificently yesterday. And so did your men. You held up an entire armored column, but of course, only for a little while, so it all was quite futile. It was too bad that all of you except two had to perish."

"That's war, I guess."

"You must have lost many friends, and I would like to extend to you my condolences."

"I wasn't that friendly with them."

"Could you tell me the nature of your mission?"

"My name is Frank Mazursky. I am a sergeant. My serial number is RA 11282203. Under the Geneva Convention, that's all I have to tell you, with all due respect, sir."

Kruger nodded. "I understand how you feel, Sergeant Mazursky, but you see, there's a problem. If you don't answer my questions, I will have to turn you over to interrogators from the SS, and they don't have very much respect for the Geneva Convention. They'll get the truth out of you one way or another, so I think it might be easier for you if you just told it to me here while you have the chance. You have heard of our SS, haven't you?"

"Yes sir."

"You don't want them to interrogate you, do you?"

"No sir."

"What was your mission on the ridge?"

"Oh, we weren't on no mission, sir. That just happened to be our position. We were sort of guarding the road, when all of a sudden we saw all those tanks coming. We didn't think we could get away, so we had to stay and fight."

"Why didn't you think you could get away? From your position, you should have seen the tanks coming from miles away' "

"But we didn't. We didn't expect any German tanks that far back. You took us by surprise."

Kruger smiled proudly. "We certainly did. We've pushed you Allies back by as much as a hundred kilometers in certain sectors. The tide of the war has changed, Sergeant Mazursky, but you needn't concern yourself about that. Your fighting days are over. You're a prisoner now.

But tell me, why were you guarding the road so far in back of your lines. It doesn't make sense to me."

"I was just following orders, sir. I just do what I'm told."

"Perhaps your headquarters knew that an attack was imminent?"

"Search me."

"I beg your pardon?"

"I said search me."

Kruger looked puzzled. "You mean you want me to search through your clothing?"

"No, that's just more slang. It means I don't know."

"Oh." Kruger leaned forward and wrote that information on his pad. Then he looked at Mazursky again. "Do you know where the rest of your company is right now?"

Mazursky wondered what information he could safely give, and what information might be harmful to the U.S. Army. "My company should be just a couple of miles to the southeast of where you found me, but if you've advanced 100 kilometers, I don't know where they are right now."

"That's where they were when you left them?"

"Yes sir."

"You're sure?"

"Yes sir."

Kruger looked coldly at him. "It is true that we have advanced all along the Ardennes front, and we've gathered information on all abandoned allied positions. Let me consult my map here." Kruger adjusted his monocle and looked at the map. He measured with a ruler. "Yes, there was a series of abandoned positions two miles southeast from the position where we found you. So that's where you were, eh?"

"Yes sir."

"When?"

"A few days ago."

"You haven't been in touch with your company since?"

"No sir."

"Not even by radio?"

"No sir."

"Didn't you think of contacting them when you saw the tanks coming?"

"I tried to, but couldn't get an answer."

"Why didn't you send a runner?"

"I figured if my company commander wanted to speak to me, he'd find a way."

"You certainly didn't show much initiative, sergeant."

"I just follow orders, sir."

"I can see from your shoulder patch that you are a member of the Eighth Corps, is that correct?"

"Yes."

"Who is the commander of the Eighth Corps, can you tell me?"

"Major General Troy H. Middleton."

"What division are you in?"

Mazursky realized he was on a tightrope. He didn't want to tell any information that the Germans didn't have, but on the other hand he didn't want to be tortured by the SS. He decided it was safe to mention the unit he was in. The main thing was not to say that they were now located outside of Dillendorf, where their mission was to defend the oil reserves stored in that town.

"The 73rd Division, sir."

"What regiment?"

"The 25th."

"Company?"

"Charlie Company, sir."

Kruger consulted his map again. "25th Regiment, eh? Hmmmm. Well, we don't know where they are. You don't have any idea where they could have gone?"

"No sir."

"Well, they're probably defending some strategic position someplace to the rear of where you were. Do you have any idea of what that might be?"

"No sir."

"Don't you know where your division headquarters was located?"

"No sir."

"Why not?"

"I didn't need to know, so I never asked."

"Again, that shows an astonishing lack of initiative, sergeant. You're a brave man, but you could never be a non-commissioned officer in the German army with your attitude."

"I don't want to be a non-commissioned officer in the German army, sir."

"Well, I wasn't offering you the position."

"Wouldn't take it anyway."

"I'm afraid you haven't been very helpful to me."

"Sorry about that."

"Isn't Mazursky a Polish name?"

"Yes."

Kruger smiled. "Very interesting."

"What's so interesting about it?"

"I was on the Polish campaign in 1939. We won easily."

"That's because you outnumbered the Poles and were better equipped. There would have been something wrong if you didn't win easily."

"Of course, I'd expect you to apologize for the Poles, since you are one yourself."

"I'm not a Pole, I'm an American. I was born in America and both of my parents were born in America."

"Yes, but what is an American? Your country is a hodgepodge of all races and cultures. America is a myth. It is just a place where the criminals of the world have congregated."

Mazursky was getting mad, because he happened to be a patriot. However he didn't want to blow his top because that might lead to the wrong end of the firing squad.

"Well," Mazursky said, "when this war is over we'll see who's a myth and who isn't."

"Indeed we shall." Kruger looked at the guard. "Take him away and bring me the other one."

Mazursky stood. "What's going to happen to me?"

"You'll be sent to a prisoner of war camp somewhere in Germany. It shouldn't be too bad. Good luck, sergeant."

"Same to you."

The guard marched Mazursky across the clearing toward the smaller tents. Mazursky hoped he hadn't given any important information away to Kruger. He wondered about the POW camp he was going to. He hoped the food wasn't too bad.

They entered the tent. The guard motioned with his gun toward Mazursky's bed. "Get back in bed."

Mazursky got back in bed while Deesing watched through his thick glasses. The guard looked at Deesing. "Come with me."

Deesing got out of bed and stretched. He was in a good mood because he had survived what he had considered to be certain death. He couldn't help thinking that perhaps he was leading a charmed life.

The guard marched him across the clearing, and Deesing sniffed the cold night air, smelling forests and gunpowder. He could hear battles raging in the distance. He thought about his home town of San Francisco, and wished he could be in one of those nice bars on Russian Hill, talking shit with some beautiful bitch.

He entered the tent, and found himself facing Lieutenant Kruger.

"Good evening, Private Deesing," Kruger said.

"Hi."

"Fuck you."

"Fuck you, too," Deesing replied before he had a chance to think about it.

Kruger smiled, pleased to have become fluent with another American slang expression. Deesing expected a rifle butt to come down on his head at any moment.

"Have a seat, Private Deesing," Kruger said.

"How come you know my name?"

"We have already been through the identification papers you carry. We know all about you and Sergeant Mazursky."

Deesing sat, and Kruger introduced himself, offered a cigarette. Deesing accepted. Kruger proceeded to interrogate Deesing in much the same manner as he'd interrogated Mazursky, and like Mazursky, Deesing divulged only useless information.

"I'm surprised by how little you know about your unit," Kruger said chidingly.

"I'm only a private. I don't have to know anything."

"Your lack of initiative is quite surprising to a German officer. We expect more from our men."

"Then how come you're losing the war?"

"Losing the war?" Kruger raised his eyebrows. "We are not losing the war!"

"Oh."

"We are winning the war!"

Deesing nodded and smiled, because he didn't want to give the appearance of being disagreeable. That might not be too healthy.

"Right now, in case you're interested," Kruger said, his voice under control once more, "we are advancing on all fronts. Soon we'll split your armies in half, encircle them, and annihilate them."

"Well, that's war," Deesing said philosophically.

"Perhaps you don't believe me?"

"Sure I believe you. I mean, why shouldn't I believe you?"

"Good. I'm glad you're so reasonable. By the way, what

kind of name is *Deesing?*"

"My father was Welsh, and my mother was German."

"Is that so?"

"Yes."

Kruger smiled and removed his monocle. "Well, that makes you half German."

"That's true."

"You're an Aryan."

"I suppose so."

"Congratulations."

"Thank you."

"Why did your mother go to America."

"She was born in America. It was her grandfather who emigrated. Nobody knows why."

"It's too bad he did. You'd be on the winning side now."

"Well, that's life."

"Do you speak German?"

"Not at all."

"What a shame."

"I suppose so."

"It's too bad you are forced to congregate with Sergeant Mazursky. He is a Pole, and they are an inferior people."

Deesing didn't know what to say, because he didn't consider Mazursky so inferior.

"You don't think so?" Kruger asked.

"Oh yes. Certainly."

"Good. I'm glad that you still think like a German despite your pollution by American life." Kruger looked at the guard. "Take him away."

"Yes sir."

Kruger looked at Deesing as the latter stood up. "Good luck to you."

"Thanks."

The German soldier marched Deesing back to the tent, where Mazursky was snoring loudly. Deesing got into bed and thought about his empty stomach. He was very hungry, but had been afraid to ask Kruger for food because he'd wanted to get away from him. It was always best to remain as inconspicuous as possible. Never volunteer for anything.

But that wasn't doing his stomach any good. Deesing had been something of a gourmet in civilian life. He'd eaten at fancy restaurants whenever he could afford it, and at home he'd prepared elaborate meals for the girls he hoped to seduce. Finally he fell asleep.

In the morning, Mazursky, Deesing, and some other prisoners were loaded onto a truck and driven away. They hadn't had any breakfast. As the sun broke on the horizon Mazursky calculated that they were moving in a northeasterly direction, deeper into Germany. They passed German villages and farmlands, crossed the Rhine, and stayed on country roads. Around noon the truck turned a bend and straight ahead was a large barbed wire camp on a plain surrounded by mountains.

The truck drove to the gate of the camp, and the prisoners were ordered by armed guards to get down. Then they were marched inside. There were rows of barracks on one side, an exercise yard, and behind a barbed wire fence, a number of administration buildings. Mazursky noticed that all the Germans in here wore the black uniforms of the SS, and a chill went up his back. He and the other prisoners were marched to the center of the yard, where a group of prisoners were already standing in ranks at attention. Mazursky's group was lined up next to the others and ordered to stand at attention.

One of the Army guards, a short husky man, addressed them. "This is the prisoner of war camp called Schwanditz. You will stand here at attention until you are dismissed. If any man leaves the formation he will be shot. That is all."

The guard marched to the administration section, an SS guard opened the gate, and he went into one of the buildings. A short while later the Army guard came out and left the camp with those soldiers who'd accompanied him in.

Mazursky watched them go ruefully, because he'd rather be in the hands of the German army than the SS. He was hungry and had a headache from his wound. The exercise yard was covered with tromped down snow and slicks of ice. He figured the temperature must be around 20 degrees, and his feet hurt from the cold. He wondered how long they'd have to stand there.

Time passed, and his legs and back ached. Some of the prisoners who were more seriously wounded collapsed onto the snow. Nobody dared pick them up. Throughout the afternoon more trucks arrived with more prisoners. By late afternoon there were several hundred prisoners in the formation. SS guards with clubs and submachine guns circled around them like jackals. None of the prisoners had eaten that day.

Near sundown, four SS officers were seen leaving a

building in the administrative area, accompanied by eight guards. The SS officers came to a stop before the group of prisoners, looked them over, laughed and joked. Finally one of them, a colonel, stepped forward, his hands on his hips. He wore shiny black boots, and on his visored cap was the death's head insignia of the SS.

"Good afternoon, prisoners," he said in a thick German accent. "I am Colonel Weber, the commandant of this camp. You are my prisoners. You are here because our counteroffensive in the west has changed the face of the war. The Allied armies are in rout before the might of the Reich. Those of you who could not run away fast enough are dead or in confinement. You did not prove to be very good soldiers, but that need not concern us here. You will sleep in those barracks behind you. You will be fed twice a day. You will do whatever work we tell you to do. If you give us any problems, we will kill you. If you try to escape, we will kill you. Anyone who strikes a guard will be killed. That is all. You may go to the barracks."

The SS men returned to their compound, and the prisoners broke formation and crossed the yard toward the barracks. Mazursky walked beside Deesing. Both had their hands in their pockets and their heads down. They felt disoriented and demoralized.

"Gee, what a fucking place," Deesing said.

"I'm damn near starved to death."

"Me too."

"We've got to get the hell out of here somehow."

"How?"

"There's got to be a way."

They entered one of the barracks. It consisted of a small amount of floor space near the door, and a huge number of double bunk beds. The prisoners would be jammed in like sardines on them.

An American lieutenant in the uniform of the Army Air Corps was sitting on the edge of his bunk as Mazursky and Deesing entered followed by other prisoners. He was a dark-haired man of average build, wearing a brown leather jacket and his visored flight cap. "Welcome to the fun house," he said sardonically. "I'm Lieutenant Wells."

Mazursky and Deesing introduced themselves, as did most of the others. The newcomers were mostly soldiers, and the prisoners already in the barracks were a mixture of Air Corps and ground troops, but mostly Air Corps.

"When do we eat," Mazursky asked.

"Oh, in a little while," Wells replied. "I can tell you what's on the menu already: bread and soup. It's the same every night. In the morning it's bread and hot water that's been flavored with chicory, and they mix sawdust with the flour, so be careful you don't get any splinters in your gums."

The newcomers crowded around the old-timers who were with Wells.

"How long you been here?" one of them asked Wells.

"Six months. I was in a bomber that was shot down near Frankfurt."

Mazursky walked away from the group and found himself a bunk on the other side of the room. Deesing followed him. Mazursky didn't look very happy.

"What's wrong?" Deesing asked.

"There's something fishy going on here."

"What do you mean?"

"I mean Wells. If he's been here six months on nothing except soup and bread with sawdust in it, he's looking awfully healthy."

"I see what you mean."

"He's probably a spy."

"Maybe we should kill him."

"What good would that do? They'd just send in another spy. The way things stand, I don't know how many of these are spies and how many aren't. The only people I'm completely sure about is me and you. We've got to get the fuck out of here, Deesing."

"I'm for that."

"Tomorrow we'll reconnoiter the area. There's got to be a weak spot."

The door to the barracks opened and two prisoners came in, carrying a cauldron of soup. Behind them was a prisoner carrying a huge basket of bread. They set down the food near the opening of the door.

"On every bunk there's a bowl and a spoon," one of them said. "Don't lose them, because you won't get anymore. All right, everybody line up and chow down!"

The men formed a twisting line and passed in front of the prisoners with the food. As Mazursky neared the head of the line he was given a chunk of brown bread, and some soup that looked like muddy water. He and Deesing moved to their bunks and dined.

"The fucking soup tastes like dishwater," Mazursky said.

"The bread is horrible."

"My boy, we're not going to last long on this."

"Like you said, tomorrow we'll have a look around."

"Yeah."

After the meal, the prisoners with the cauldron and basket returned to the mess, while the others licked their bowls and spoons clean.

Suddenly the front door of the barracks burst open and three guards marched in. They carried clubs and submachine guns.

"Hello American soldiers," said a big burly one with a scar on his cheek. "I am your guard and my name is Corporal Blomberg. Soon we will put the lights out, and you will go to sleep. No one is permitted outside after the lights go out. If any of you are found outside, you will be shot. Understand?"

"What if we have to go to the bathroom?" one of the prisoners asked.

"You must go before the lights go out."

"What time do the lights go out?"

"In two hours. You will be awakened early in the morning by the sound of a whistle. There will be a formation in front of the barracks. Then there will be breakfast. Then you will be marched to work. You are not here on vacation, you know. That is all. Have a nice sleep, and watch out for the bedbugs." He laughed, and left with his companions.

The men meandered out the latrine, which was a stinking hole in the ground with a roof over it, and returned to the barracks to sit around the little coal stove from which a slight bit of heat emanated.

Wells was being very friendly, slapping other prisoners on their backs and telling jokes to cheer them up. He sat next to one of the prisoners, who was no more than eighteen years old.

"Hiya feller," Wells said.

"Hello Lieutenant," the soldier replied, uneasy in the presence of an officer.

Wells noticed the discomfort. "Relax. Take it easy. We're all in this mess together, right?"

"I guess so, sir."

"What's your name?"

"O'Grady."

"Where you from?"

"Philadelphia."

"No kidding? I was in Philadelphia once on business. Nice town."

"I sure wish I was there now."

"I don't blame you. What outfit were you with, anyway?"

"Third Armored Division."

"A tanker, huh?"

"Yes sir."

"You were actually in a tank crew?"

"Yes sir."

"What was your job?"

"I was a gunner, sir."

"Where were you captured?"

"Near Ermsdorf, sir."

"What regiment were you in?"

"The eighteenth."

"Where were you headed when you were captured?"

"We were on our way to —"

Mazursky, who happened to be a few feet away,

smacked the private on the shoulder and smiled, interrupting him. "Hey soldier, you know better than that."

"Huh?" the private asked, surprised.

"I said you know better than that."

"Better than what?"

"You shouldn't be talking about things like that. Why, the Germans might be right outside the door listening. You shouldn't give out information that might be useful to the enemy in a place where the enemy might overhear you." Mazursky turned his big brown eyes on Lieutenant Wells. "I'm surprised at you, sir, asking the boy questions like that."

Wells looked a little nervous. "I didn't think there was any harm in it."

"Locations of military units and their probable direction might be useful to the enemy, don't you think so?"

"Perhaps you're right, sergeant."

Mazursky stood up and raised his voice. "All you men be careful of what you say around here! Don't say anything that might be of use to the enemy! A loose tongue might mean that some of your buddies might die!"

Somebody laughed. "Aw, come on, Sarge. We don't need any chickenshit here."

Mazursky looked in the direction of the voice. It was a light-haired corporal with the insignia of the Second Division on his shoulder. He was a little taller and broader than Mazursky, and Mazursky wondered if he was a spy too.

"We're all still in the Army," Mazursky said. "We have to be careful of giving information to the enemy."

"Shit, Sarge. Nobody's listening."

"You never know." Mazursky didn't like to call attention to himself this way, but somebody had to step forward and take charge.

"I bet if we went outside right now, nobody would be listening."

"They might have a hidden microphone someplace, or worse than that, somebody in here might be a planted spy."

"Huh?" the corporal said not very convincingly, and in that moment Mazursky figured he was a spy.

"I said anybody here might be a spy. None of us knows anybody else. It could happen."

The corporal stood up. "I think you're full of shit, Sarge."

"I think you'd better respect these three stripes on my sleeve, soldier. We're all still in the Army."

"Fuck you, Sarge." The corporal smiled like a wise guy.

"If we ever get out of this, asshole, you're going to find yourself before a court martial for insubordination."

"Who are calling an asshole?"

"You."

"You can't talk to me that way!"

"I just did, asshole."

The corporal looked around excitedly. "I'm sick of taking shit from you goddamn sergeants. We're all prisoners now, and rank doesn't mean anything as far as I'm concerned. Another word out of you, and I'm going to go over there and kick your ass."

"You and who else?"

"Me and me alone."

"Anytime you feel froggy, go ahead and jump."

The Corporal stormed across the floor, his fists in the air. Mazursky raised his own fists and came out at him, dancing lightly on the balls of his feet. Mazursky had been a regimental boxer and won a few championships. They met in the middle of the floor. Mazursky bobbed and weaved, wanting the corporal to throw the first punch so he'd have the excuse to kick his ass.

The corporal threw a left jab, and Mazursky ducked under it easily. When he came up, he threw a hard punch at the corporal's stomach. The corporal doubled over, clutching his gut, and Mazursky hooked him hard twice, shot an uppercut that straightened him up, and then threw a haymaker that sent the corporal flying across the floor. Mazursky went after him like a wild man, and pummeled the corporal to the floor. The corporal lay bleeding from his mouth and nose.

Mazursky stood over him, his fists at his side. "Is there anybody else who thinks he can kick the ass of a sergeant?"

Nobody answered.

"Anybody know this asshole corporal?"

Most of the men shook their heads. Nobody stepped forward.

Mazursky shrugged his shoulders and walked toward his bunks. "Then I guess the fucker is going to have to lay there."

Deesing slapped his on the shoulder. "Nice going, Sarge!"

Mazursky grunted, because he didn't think the going was so nice. If that corporal was really a spy, there'd probably be trouble tomorrow. Mazursky wished the fight hadn't been necessary, but somebody had to stop the loose talk.

The lights went out in the barracks and everybody went to bed. That is, everybody except Mazursky. He crept to the window and looked outside. Guards walked around outside the barbed wire, and on high towers there were machine guns and searchlights that crossed back and forth over the barracks and the yard.

"What are you looking for, sergeant?" Lieutenant Wells asked.

"Just looking."

"You wouldn't be thinking of escaping, would you?"

"Who me? Naw, I don't think anybody could get out of here."

"If you decide to try, let me know. I'd sure like to go with you."

"I'll sure tell you, sir. You can rely on it."

Mazursky returned to his bunk, but lay with his eyes open, ready for trouble. The beaten corporal dragged himself off the floor and went to bed. Soon there was snoring. Some of the men, in the grip of combat nightmares, screamed for mortar support, asked for more ammunition, or just howled in terror. After a while Mazursky slipped down from his bunk and knelt beside Deesing, who was fast asleep.

Mazursky nudged him. "Wake up!" he whispered in Deesing's ear.

Deesing awoke with a jolt. "What's happening!" Since becoming a front line soldier, he always expected the worst.

"Listen to me," Mazursky whispered. "I've got a feeling

something bad is going to happen to me tomorrow. If they don't kill me, and if they just take me away, try to find out where I am, and come see me, understand?"

"Okay."

"Go back to sleep."

Mazursky crawled back up to his bunk, closed his eyes, and wondered what the morning would bring.

Chapter
Six

THE WHISTLES BLEW and the front door of the barracks was thrown open. A group of guards led by the one with the scarred face stormed in and began throwing men out of their bunks.

"Wake up, American soldiers!" Scarface shouted. "Everybody outside!"

Scarface grabbed Mazursky by the front of his jacket and pulled him out of bed, letting him go at the last crucial moment so Mazursky would fall painfully to the floor. Mazursky wanted to kick the bastard into hamburger, but the consequences of that act would be too hideous to contemplate. Instead he brushed himself off and walked out the door to the formation.

All the prisoners in the camp stood in ranks in the yard and were counted by the guards as the sun made a faint glow on the still cloudy horizon. A young SS Lieutenant with the face of a baby told them that after breakfast there would be another formation. Mazursky deliberately stood in one of the rear ranks, so he could keep an eye on the corporal he'd beaten up last night.

After the formation was dismissed, Mazursky stood in the shadows of the barracks as the corporal, after looking furtively around, walked back to the latrines, talking in low tones with Lieutenant Wells and two privates.

Mazursky followed them, took a crap, and washed up. He saw the corporal and some other men walking toward the administration compound. Mazursky sidled up to one of the old time prisoners. "Where are they going?" he asked.

'To get the food."

Then Mazursky remembered that the corporal had been one of the ones who'd brought the soup and bread last night. So that was how they passed on their messages. They just went over to the main kitchen and waiting for them were guards to whom they passed on information. Mazursky was more sure than ever that he was in for hard times.

He and the others went to the barracks, and after a while the corporal and his cohorts showed up with the morning's bread and coffee. Everyone got in line like the night before for their morning rations, then sat and dipped the tasteless bread into the so-called coffee.

"I see you're still here," Deesing said below his breath as he sat beside Mazursky.

"But not for long, I don't think. These barracks are crawling with spies, and I'm sure that corporal is one of them. He passes his information on when he goes to pick up the food. At the next formation, I'm sure they're going to call me out."

"The moral of this story," Deesing said, "is to keep your fucking mouth shut from now on."

"It's too late for that, and besides, somebody had to step forward."

"No, they didn't. So what if the Germans pick up a little information? It's no skin off your ass. We're going to win the war anyway. The Germans don't stand a chance."

"You don't pass information to the enemy. That's one of the rules of war."

"I didn't pass any information on. And neither did you."

"But I'm a non-commissioned officer, and I can't let anybody else do it either."

Deesing shook his head. "You fucking regular army soldiers are all fanatics."

"We just take things a little more seriously than you fucking draftees."

"But we're prisoners now. Nothing matters anymore. We're out of the ballgame."

"You're not out of the ballgame until you're dead, Deesing. Remember that."

"Okay, Sarge."

Mazursky looked up and noticed the corporal glowering at him. His face was badly bruised and he couldn't get hospital attention because that would blow his cover as a spy. Mazursky could see the loathing in his eyes, but also a touch of triumph. Mazursky knew his goose was cooked.

After breakfast, the whistle blew. The men piled out and got into formation. It was brighter out now, but there was still a thick cloud cover. Mazursky wondered whether the Allies had stopped the German attack without the aid of the Air Corps. He took his place in the formation, as dread crept over his body and penetrated his mind. What if the Allies lost the war? He gritted his teeth. That could not be permitted to happen.

The formation was similar to formations in the peacetime Army, where there'd be four ranks of men in front of each barracks. Before Mazursky's formation there were an SS officer and a dozen guards. Mazursky looked out the corner of his eyes to other formations, and heard the SS men screaming and hollering at the prisoners.

In front of Mazursky's formation, the SS officer and guards were looking at the prisoners, mumbling among themselves. Then they started walking around the formation toward the back where Mazursky was standing in the last rank. Although it was twenty-five degrees that morning, sweat broke out on his forehead as they approached him. He heard them stop behind him. Two of the guards grabbed him by the arms and turned him around so that he faced another SS guard.

The guard punched Mazursky in the mouth, and Mazursky's head snapped back. The lights went out for a few seconds. They came back on and Mazursky straightened his head. The guard punched him again, and Mazursky felt his lips rip against his teeth. Groggy, he felt the two guards dragging him across the exercise yard.

Halfway across it, he regained consciousness fully. He tasted blood and felt the pain of his cut lips. He heard more guards marching behind him. He wondered if they were going to kill him.

They took him to the administration compound, and a guard opened the gate to admit them. He was dragged through the alleys between the wooden buildings and soon they came to a long squat building surrounded by guards and barbed wire. The only widows were in the front of the building.

A guard opened the barbed wire gate and Mazursky was dragged up the steps, through the door, and into an orderly room, where some SS guards were sitting around on benches or behind desks. This was the only room of the building that had windows. The guards spoke German to each other and threw hostile glances at Mazursky, who was still held by his arms, dripping blood onto his field jacket. Then one of them took keys and opened a door at the rear of the orderly room. Mazursky was dragged behind them into a cold darker corridor lined with tiny cells. Mazursky peered through the darkness and saw men huddling in the cells, their eyes gleaming. Halfway down the corridor a cell door was unlocked and Mazursky was thrown into it. The door was locked behind him.

The guards stood on the other side of the bars and glowered at him. "If you make any trouble in here, American, we will shoot you," one of them said. Then they turned and walked away.

Mazursky looked around his cell. In the dimness he could perceive a wooden cot bolted to the wall and a slop bucket in the corner. There was no mattress on the cot. There was no heat in the cell. The air smelled faintly of piss and shit. His head ached and he knew the bandage should be changed. It occurred to him that this was the worst off he'd ever been in his life. He sat on the cot and leaned back against the wall. He hoped they wouldn't keep him there too long, because he was afraid he might go out of his mind. The cell was only eight by six, and he knew they didn't show movies.

He heard the guards leave the cell area and slam the door behind them. Then he heard movement and muffled voices in the cells around him. There were probably spies in here too. He'd have to be careful. If only he could be home eating a plate of his mother's pirogen and drinking a bottle of Knickerbocker Beer.

"What's your name, fella?" asked a voice in the cell to the left.

Mazursky got up and stood by the bars in front of his own cell. "Mazursky."

"What's your rank?"

"Sergeant. Who're you?"

"Sergeant Bull Moose Dexter, of the Seventh Cav." He had a New England accent. "What outfit were you with?"

"The 25th Infantry Regiment."

"No kidding? An old buddy of mine is with the 25th. He's a mess sergeant, with George Company of the 2nd Battalion. Name's Fenwick, Arthur Fenwick. Ever hear of him?"

"Artie Fenwick? Sure I know him. I used to drink with him from time to time at the NCO Club in Fort Benning. How do you know him?"

"We were in boot camp together at Fort Leonard Wood, and kept bumping into each other ever since. The Army's a small place once you've been in it for awhile."

"Ain't that the truth."

"What're you in here for?"

Mazursky hesitated to tell him, because he thought

Dexter might be a spy. It was possible that the Germans had Fenwick a prisoner someplace, and had found out that he'd been in boot camp at Fort Leonard Wood.

"I don't know what I'm in here for," Mazursky said.

"How can you not know what you're in here for?"

"I don't know. They just pulled me out of formation and brought me here."

"You must have done something."

"I guess so, but I don't know what it was."

"When'd you get here?"

"Yesterday. How about you?"

"Three days ago."

"What'd you do to get put in here?"

"They thought I was planning to escape," Dexter said.

"Were you?"

"What do you think?"

"How the fuck should I know?"

"Well I was. I got a few people together to break out with me, and one of them must have been a spy, because the next thing I knew I was thrown in this cell."

"How do you know I'm not a spy?" Mazursky asked.

"Are you?"

"If I were, do you think I'd tell you?"

"No. But I don't think you are."

"Why not?"

"Because what could a spy find out in here? This is where all the hardasses are, the guys who make trouble out in the camp. This is where they put us on ice so we won't make any more trouble. They know they'll never get anything out of us except a hard time, so they lock us in here and hope we'll die, which we probably will because from what I've seen so far, the rations ain't much. Just a piece of bread in the morning and another piece of bread at night, with a cup of water each time. We won't last long on that."

"About a couple of weeks, I guess. Is there any way to get out of here?"

"Not unless you've got a gun, and I doubt if even that would be enough."

"Do they ever let us out for a little air?"

"The only way to get out of here is on a stretcher."

"You could pretend to be sick," Mazursky said.

"If you get sick, they keep you right where you are. They only take you out on a stretcher when you're dead."

"Don't look too good, does it?"

"Fuck no."

"What are you going to do about it?"

"I ain't going to do nothing about it, because there ain't nothing to do."

"There's got to be something."

"When you find out what it is, let me know, okay?"

"Okay."

Mazursky looked around his cell. Possibly he could bore his way through one of the walls, but there were barbed wire and guards outside. You couldn't dig your way out because the building was on stilts and the guards could see underneath it. Maybe there was no way out. Maybe he was going to starve to death in this little fucking cell.

"You still there?" Dexter said.

"Yeah."

"What did you say you were in here for?"

"I didn't say."

"Well, why don't you say?"

"I hit a guy last night."

"What the fuck for?"

"The guy was a spy."

"Oh, so that's why you've got spies on the brain."

"That's right."

"So have I. They're everywhere."

"Maybe even in here."

"I don't think so. If you were a spy, would you want to be locked up in here on bread and water, without any heat."

"No, but I'm not a spy."

"I don't think any spy would, and besides, what are they going to figure out from guys like us?"

"Nothing I guess. But if you start asking me about where my regiment is, I'm going to kill you first chance I get."

"I don't give a fuck where your regiment is. They're probably back in Belgium by now anyway. Those Germans were pushing hard when they overran my company, and there were a whole of them. They tore a big hole in our line where we were, and I imagine they did the same thing where you were."

"Stop trying to get information out of me, you Nazi cocksucker!"

"I'm not trying to get information out of you."

"Oh yes you are!"

"I think you'd better lie down."

"Who can lie down on that slab of wood over there?"

"You'll get used to it."

Mazursky sat on his wooden slab and rested his chin in his hand. Around him he could hear prisoners mumbling like he and Dexter were. He wondered if Dexter was a spy. He wondered if it mattered if Dexter was a spy. He thought about the Second Platoon and all his buddies who'd been killed on the Dillendorf Road.

"Hey Mazursky," Dexter hissed.

"What?"

"Where you from?"

"Mazursky got up and leaned against the bars again. "New York City."

"No wonder you're such an asshole."

"Where you from?"

"A little town in Maine called Houlton. Ever hear of it?"

"I don't know anything about little hick towns."

"It ain't no little hick town."

"It'd have to be if you came from there."

"You guys from New York think you know everything."

"At least we're not corny like you hicks."

"What'd you do before you joined the Army?" Dexter asked.

"I didn't do anything. That was during the Depression."

"What'd you do for food?"

"Scrounged around, mostly. What did you do?"

"I was a lumberjack."

"Oh, you must be a tough guy, huh?"

"I can take care of myself."

"Then what're you doing in here?"

"Fuck you, Mazursky."

"Up your ass, Dexter."

"You guys from New York make me sick."

"You corny bastard. You stump jumper."

"You horse's ass."

"You scumbag."

Mazursky spent the rest of the afternoon pacing his cell, arguing with Dexter, and worrying about his bleak future. He became hungry, but the hunger became a dull ache that he got used to. There had to be a way to break out of this joint.

The doors opened and he heard a commotion in the hall. Pressing his head against the bars, he peered down the corridor but couldn't see anything for a while, and then the guards came into view, pushing a wagon on which was the water and bread. When they were abreast of his cell they gave him a chunk of bread no bigger than a fist, and a wooden cup of water.

"Don't lose that cup," the guard said, "because it's the only one you'll ever get."

Mazursky sat on the cot and ate the bread slowly to make it last. Then he washed it down with water, saving half the cup in case he got thirsty later. His hunger still wasn't satisfied. He'd rather be on the front lines dodging mortar shells than in this miserable situation. He began to feel lonely. He walked to the bars.

"Hey Dexter?"

"Yeah?"

"What're you doing?"

"I was thinking about jerking off. What're you doing?"

"What could I be doing?"

"Are you married, Mazursky?"

"Not now."

"You mean you don't want to talk about it now?"

"I mean that I used to be married, but that I'm not married now. Are you married?"

"Yes. Her name's Trudy. She was a good old gal."

"I wonder who's fucking her right now."

"You son of a bitch!"

"What's the matter?"

"What a rotten fucking thing to say."

"You don't think somebody is fucking her right now? Are you kidding? What do you think she's doing? Twiddling her thumbs and waiting for you to come home? She probably thinks you're missing in action, probably dead, and you know she's not going to let her cooze go to waste."

"Mazursky, if we ever get out of here, I'm going to whip your fucking ass."

"Look at it logically. You're sitting here horny as a billy-goat and she's sitting up there in Maine horny as a cat in heat. Some big handsome 4-F lumberjack who's probably smarter than you puts her hand on his cock, and what's she going to do? Say no? Are you kidding? Would you say no if some babe took off her dress in front of you right now."

"What a lowlife you are, Mazursky."

"Who me?"

"I take back what I said before. I'm not going to whip

your ass when we get out of here. I'm going to kill you."

"You're full of shit, you stump jumper bastard. If you ever come near me, I'll kick your ass."

"I can't wait to get my hands on you."

"Some fucking gorilla has got his hands all over your wife right now, you bastard. And she's probably chewing on his cock."

"You bastard."

"You cornball."

Mazursky heard Dexter walk back from the bars of his cell, so Mazursky returned to his cot and sat down. He didn't like to needle Dexter that way, but what else was there to do? At least it had been a little excitement. He'd been able to forget his predicament for a few minutes. But now it back with him again. He was trapped like a rat and he knew it. There was no way out of this one. He looked at his trusty old Bulova; it was 1800 hours. He wished he had a cigar. He wished he'd never joined the Army.

He lay down on his cot, put his hands behind his head, and closed his eyes. After a while he heard a faint rumbling in the distance. He sat up and listened. It was a bombardment. A bombardment? Either the Allies had advanced and mounted an artillery attack, or the weather was clear and the Air Corps had gone into action.

Mazursky doubted if the Allied armies could have advanced this far. It must be the Air Corps bombing targets in the area.

"Hey Mazursky, you hear that?" asked Dexter.

"Yeah, the weather must have cleared."

"It's music to my ears."

"If the weather stays clear, we'll push the Krauts all the way back to Berlin."

"What do you mean, we?"

"The Allies. I hope they get here fast so they can let us out of here."

"I don't think they'll reach here for quite a while. There are a lot of Germans between here and our front lines."

"How do you know where our front lines are? They might be five miles away."

"Don't be such an asshole all your life, Mazursky. They couldn't have moved up so fast."

"I hope they drop a bomb right on that fucking Hitler."

"If I could get my hands on that son of a bitch I'd tear his head off. Do you realize how many people have died because of him?"

"They say he chews rugs."

"I heard he eats shit."

"I heard he's a queer."

"All those big shot Nazis are queers."

"The Germans have got to be the most fucked-up people in the world. I mean, who else would take a person like Adolf Hitler seriously."

"They're good soldiers though."

"We're better."

"The American soldier is the best soldier in the world."

Mazursky looked at his watch; it was 1930 hours. "I'm going to bed, Dexter. Have a nice night."

"You too, Mazursky. Watch out for the rats."

"What rats?"

"You'll find out."

DOOM PLATOON

Mazursky went to his cot and lay down. Now he had something new to worry about. Rats. If only he had been a 4-F.

Somehow he had to figure out a way to escape from that camp.

Chapter Seven

IN THE MORNING after breakfast a troop of armed guards entered the cell block and opened the doors.

'EVERYBODY OUT!"

In the corridor, Mazursky saw Dexter for the first time. He was broad shouldered, lumpy-faced, and had a broken nose.

"What's going on?" Mazursky asked him.

"How the fuck should I know?"

"You've been here longer than me. I thought you might know a few things."

"NO TALKING!"

They were marched outside into the cold dawn, and then to the exercise yard of the camp. Across the yard were the regular prisoners in front of their barracks. Mazursky felt weak and dizzy as he stood beside Dexter in the formation. We wondered what was going on.

An SS officer and some guards stood at the front of the formation.

"You are going out on a work detail," the officer

144

shouted, his hands on his hips. "Anyone who does not do his share of work will be killed. Anyone who tries to escape will be killed. Anyone who talks without proper authorization will be killed. We are not going to play silly games with you foolish Americans. If you give us any problems we will kill you and that will be that." He turned to the guards. "Take them away."

The regular prisoners, under heavy guard, were marched out of the camp first, and then came the special group of prisoners that included Mazursky and Dexter. They walked down a dirt road to a paved road, and then walked on it past farmhouses, meadows, and forests. A mist rose from the snow on the ground, and the trees looked eerie and twisted in the dawn light. As they marched, the day grew brighter. Mazursky wondered where they were going.

At 0800 hours they approached a military installation and marched through the front gates. They passed barracks and mess halls that had been damaged by bombing, and then came to an air field that was all torn up. Mazursky realized this must have been one of the targets of the allied bombing last night. He was proud of the Air Corps.

Picks and shovels were distributed, and the prisoners were ordered to fill in the holes on the air strip. Trucks filled with dirt and gravel emptied their loads near the holes, and the prisoners shoveled the fill in. Guards with submachine guns stood around, some with big dogs who liked to snarl and bare their teeth at the prisoners. Mazursky worked next to Dexter and kept looking around for possibilities to escape. If only they could get one of those trucks. He noticed that the trucks were driven by ordinary soldiers, not SS men.

At noon a different kind of truck arrived, this one carrying soup and bread for the noon meal. Mazursky decided that this work detail wasn't so bad, because at least you got more to eat. He stood in line with Dexter and got a bowl of soup and chunk of bread. Then he sat down with Dexter and ate in the midst of a group of prisoners. Guards and dogs patrolled the perimeter of the group.

"How can we got one of those trucks?" Mazursky asked in a low voice.

"I'm working on it," Dexter replied, dipping his bread into his soup.

"There's got to be some way."

"There's always a way. We'll just have to figure it out."

After lunch, they all went back to work. Mazursky realized it was impossible to steal one of the trucks. There were too many guards around. They guards would shoot you down before you even got near the truck, and the dogs would eat you alive before you hit the ground.

The trucks kept coming and going all afternoon, emptying fill which the prisoners shoveled into the holes. Whenever a hole was filled it was covered with concrete. The airfield was a mass of concrete patches; there had been many bombing raids already, and Mazursky hoped the weather would remain clear so there'd be more.

At dusk the prisoners were marched back to the camp and locked in their cells. The normal evening meal of bread and water was passed around, and then the prisoners were left alone for the night.

"I don't know how much longer I can make it on these rations," Dexter said. "I can barely lift the fucking shovel out there."

"Go tell it to the chaplain."

"You're such a prick, Mazursky."

"I've been thinking about those trucks. Just as we unload them at the air strip, there must be a place where somebody loads them, right? A gravel pit or something?"

"Right."

"Somehow we've got to get on that detail."

"Why?"

"Because it might be easier to steal a truck that way."

"Why don't you go see the camp commandant and put in for a transfer?"

"Fuck you, Dexter."

"Up your ass, Mazursky."

"I bet eight guys are gang banging your wife right now."

"Your mother works in a whorehouse."

Exhausted, Mazursky went to bed. He tried to think of ways to escape but sleep overtook him. Then there was noise and shouting in the corridor. He looked at his watch, and it was morning again. They had breakfast and then were marched to the air base, where they worked all day. Then they were marched back to the prisoner of war camp for dinner and sleep.

This schedule was repeated for three more days. On the third night Mazursky lay in bed after dinner and wondered how long he could continue. The insufficient rations were making him weak and he could barely wield his shovel during the day. When he could no longer work, they'd shoot him for sure. He couldn't let that happen. But what could he do? Fighting off sleep, he thought through the problem. He realized there was one possibility, and it was a long shot. But he'd have to take it. Arising he went to the front of his cell.

"Hey Dexter!"

There was no answer.

"Dexter!"

"What is it?" Dexter asked sleepily.

"Come here, I want to talk to you."

"Lemme sleep."

"It's important."

He heard Dexter get out of bed and shuffle to his bars. "What is it, you asshole?"

"I've figured out a way to get out of here."

"What is it?"

"Well, it's not the greatest idea in the world, but the way I look at it, it's the only chance we've got. We're going to get a couple of sub-machine guns off those guards and fight our way off that air base."

"Are you fucking crazy?"

"Have you got a better idea?"

"Well, no."

"We have to do something soon, because a few more days on those rations and we're going to be dropping like flies out there. Then they'll just shoot us. We have to take a chance. There are no two ways about it."

"Maybe you're right. How can we get those machine guns?"

"I don't think that part will be too hard. You and I will

both be carrying shovels tomorrow, right? And you've probably noticed that some of those guards get a little lackadaisical out there, right? So you and I, while putting in our honest day's work, will sort of get close to one of those lackadaisical guards. At the right moment, I'll swing my shovel at his head and you grab for his submachine gun. Then you start firing at the nearest guards. I'll grab a submachine gun from a dead guard and we'll fight our way to one of those trucks. Then we'll get in and drive the fuck out of there."

"Just like that."

"Why not?"

"Because those other guards will just chop us right the fuck down."

"Not if the other prisoners are tipped off, and do the same thing we do at the same time."

There was silence for a few moments. Then Dexter said, "Hey, I think you've got something there."

"You pass the word to the guy on the other side of you, and I'll pass it to the guy on the other side of me. We'll do it at 1600 hours tomorrow, just before the workday is over. It'll be night soon after that, and maybe we'll have a better chance to get away at night."

"You think of everything, Mazursky, but there's just one thing. What if there's a spy in here?"

"I don't think there is, but if there is, what can they do to us that they're not doing already?"

"They can shoot us."

"They're going to do that anyway in a few days after we can't work anymore."

"I guess we've got to take the chance."

"You're fucking right we do."

Mazursky and Dexter moved to the cells adjacent to them and told the escape plans to the prisoners there. The prisoners were reluctant at first, but soon saw the logic of the plan. They realized it was their only hope. They had nothing to lose.

The escape plan slowly made its way around the cell block. Tomorrow at 1600 hours, when Mazursky crowned a guard with his shovel, they would try to fight their way to freedom. They were all desperate, they had nothing to lose, they were marked for death anyway.

Among them was Private Alvarro Lopez from Los Angeles, a slender weasel of a man and a skilled knife fighter who had killed three men before he joined the Army, and had never been caught. Lopez liked to kill close up, and see the expression on his opponent's face as the knife went in. He loved the feeling of triumph as his opponent fell dead at his feet. He was in special detention because he had been caught trying to grind his spoon into a knife.

Also there was Private Mike Grogan of Des Moines, Iowa, a brutal saloon fighter who liked to stomp on his victims, and who once had served a prison term for assault and battery. He was in special detention for stealing food.

In a corner cell was Private Harold Karashevsky of Portland, Oregon, an odd withdrawn man with deep set eyes, who once had been arrested for rape, but released for insufficient evidence. The Germans locked him up because they thought he was crazy, and they were right.

Next to Karashevsky was Lieutenant William Doyle of

the Army Air Corps. Doyle had been a star quarterback for the University of Michigan during his college days, had flown a P-51 Mustang on numerous combat missions over France and Germany, and was locked in a cell because he'd been caught trying to escape on two occasions. He expected a firing squad at any moment, so was most interested in the escape plan.

Also worthy of mention was Sergeant Okie Jones of Lebanon, Missouri, who had won the Congressional Medal of Honor on the Salerno beach for attacking a German pillbox single-handedly, and winning. Like Mazursky, he was locked up for beating up a spy.

Mazursky didn't know any of these men, of course, But he'd seem them all during the work detail that day and thought that they looked like the type of men who'd give a good account of themselves in a tight situation.

Tomorrow he'd find out for sure.

Chapter Eight

T HE SOUNDS OF BOMBARDMENTS reverberated throughout the night, as Allied planes dropped tons of bombs on German targets. Bright and early in the morning the prisoners at Schwanditz were awakened, fed, and marched across the countryside to the air base five miles away.

Upon arriving, Mazursky saw that the air strip had been devastated the night before. There was much work to do, and three trucks were already there waiting to be unloaded. Mazursky and the men from his detention barracks set to work unloading one of the trucks, and men from the other barracks unloaded the other trucks. Throughout the morning they shoveled dirt into the holes and attempted to level off the landing strip. At noon they paused to eat, and Mazursky sat next to Dexter, dunking his bread into the watery soup and looking over the men from his barracks. Some appeared nonchalant, others tense and nervous. They looked like a good crew.

After lunch the work resumed. Mazursky's leaden arms

jabbed his shovel into the ground and came up with dirt, which he threw into a bomb crater. During his work he checked out the guards. None of them was paying too much attention; some chatted with each other, their gun butts on their hips and barrels pointing into the sky. Others watched the work through glassy bored eyes. The guard duty had become routine for them, and they didn't expect anything. Even the dogs were getting lazy.

The afternoon hours passed slowly. Mazursky decided to zero in on a young SS guard who had a poetic face and liked to look at sky. This guard didn't look very husky in his black SS overcoat, he was pale, and Mazursky figured that the SS must be lowering its standards if it took youths like that. Mazursky winked at Dexter, and together they worked toward that SS guard. It was drawing close to 1600 hours.

The other prisoners, seeing what Mazursky and Dexter were up to, made way for them. The sun was sinking in the west. They were unloading a truckload of dirt. Some of the prisoners were on the bed of the truck shoveling the dirt onto the ground, and other prisoners were shoveling it into a bomb crater. Three guards were watching that truck load. A short distance away a different detail from the special detention barracks was unloading another truck.

Everyone was watching Mazursky and Dexter out of the corners of their eyes as Mazursky and Dexter drew close to the scrawny guard. The guard didn't seem to notice they were only a shovel's length away; he was looking at clouds racing across the sky and thinking of his girl friend in Berlin. Other prisoners maneuvered closer to the other guards.

"NOW!" screamed Mazursky, as he lunged the blade of his shovel toward the guard's neck.

The guard looked down from the clouds, from the images of his girl friend, and for a split second saw the shovel streaking toward his throat. The blade of the shovel severed his throat and jugular, and the guard crumpled toward the ground as Dexter grabbed the submachine gun out of his hands, rammed a round into the chamber, clicked off the safety, and spun around, as blood sprayed over his uniform.

The other prisoners were grappling with the two other guards. Dexter ran toward the truck, with Mazursky right behind him. Guards at another truck fifty yards away noticed the unusual activity and brought their submachine guns up. Dexter opened fire on them as he ran, cutting one down and wounding another.

Lieutenant Doyle and Private Lopez both had submachine guns now, and they ran toward the truck too, firing at the other guards. Dexter jumped into the cab of the truck and saw the driver cowering behind the wheel. Dexter whacked him over the head with the barrel of his submachine gun, pushed him over, and got behind the wheel.

Mazursky got into the cab via the other door, kicked the driver onto the floor, took the submachine gun lying beside Dexter, and fired a burst at the other guards, who were rushing toward the truck. The other prisoners were lying on the ground, trying to stay out of the line of fire. Private Lopez, running toward the back of the truck, was stopped by a submachine gun burst across his stomach, and fell to the ground. Sergeant Okie Jones, himself on the run, picked the submachine gun out of Lopez's hands, and running in a zigzag toward the rear of the truck, fired at and brought down the guard who'd killed Lopez.

Private Mike Grogan caught a bullet in the head as he was trying to climb onto the bed of the truck. He fell back, and was passed by Sergeant Jones, Lieutenant Doyle and Private Karashevsky, who jumped onto the bed, pulled up the rear gate, and, kneeling behind the metal walls of the truck, sprayed bullets at the guards running toward them as the truck began to move away.

Dexter rammed the accelerator to the floor. The truck engine whinnied like a horse and the truck sped over the airstrip apron toward the nearest road. Luftwaffe pilots and ground crews came out of nearby barracks to see what was going on, but were sent scurrying for cover by submachine gun bursts from Mazursky, Jones, and Doyle. The guards at the airstrip were each down on one knee, firing at the retreating truck.

A lucky shot hit Private Karashevsky on his forehead, and ripped the top of his head off. He went flying backwards, his brains splattering Sergeant Jones and Lieutenant Doyle.

They were speeding on the road to the front gate of the air base now, and the airstrip was out of range. Jones and Doyle lay down in the dirt on the bottom of the bed, while in the front seat, Dexter steered around corners and Mazursky was putting on the jacket and hat of the German soldier on the floor of the cab. The winter sun was setting on the horizon.

Dexter drove out the front gate of the camp and soon they were on a lonely country road. In the distance they could hear the sounds of sirens.

"Head east," Mazursky said.

"There's no fucking road going east!"

"If you come to one, take it."

In the gathering twilight Mazursky spotted a narrow dirt road up ahead.

"Take that road," he said, pointing.

"Make up your fucking mind, will you?"

"Do you hear those sirens?"

"Of course I hear those sirens."

"In five minutes the Krauts will have every available vehicle swarming over these roads. We've got to get out of sight."

Dexter slowed up and turned onto the narrow dirt road. Branches scratched along the side of the truck. It was almost completely dark now.

"Don't turn on your lights whatever you do."

"What do you think I am—stupid?"

"I won't answer that. Stop after you get in about fifty yards."

"What the hell for?"

"Because we have to go back and cover up our tracks so that the Germans won't know that we've turned onto this road, dipshit."

Dexter stopped the truck. Mazursky got out and walked to the back. "Let's go," he called to Jones and Doyle. "We've got to go back and cover our tracks."

They jumped out of the rear of the truck and ran back

to the road, where they took branches and obscured their tracks with snow and mud. While they were working they heard an approaching vehicle. Hiding behind trees, they peeked at the German *kubelwagen* as it sped past. Then they came out of hiding, finished obscuring their tracks, and returned to the truck.

Dexter drove the truck deeper into the woods, until the road narrowed so much he couldn't go any farther. By then it was night, with a half moon and the milky way shining overhead. It would be a good night for bombing, and Mazursky hoped that would impede the krauts who were searching for them.

"I can't go any farther," Dexter said.

"Drive right into the woods as far as you can go. Turn left there between those trees."

Dexter didn't ask any questions; he knew Mazursky wanted to hide the truck so that it couldn't be spotted from the air. He steered between the trees, drove and skidded for twenty feet, and finally could go no further. He stopped the truck and turned off the engine.

Mazursky dragged the unconscious German soldier out of the front seat, took off all his clothes, and slit his throat. Then he put on the German's helmet and clothes over his own clothes as Dexter, Lieutenant Doyle, and Sergeant Okie Jones clustered around him.

Doyle was a short man with black hair and lively eyes. He wore a leather flight jacket and his visored officer's hat. Jones was tall and gawky, a typical farm boy from the Ozark Mountains.

"I think we should split up," Doyle said, taking charge.

"We'll have a better chance that way. What do you guys think?"

Jones spat at the snow. "I don't think we'll have much of a chance no matter what we do. If the Krauts don't get us, the starvation will."

"Oh, I don't know about that," Mazursky said. "There must be something to eat in these woods, and we might even run into a farmhouse someplace."

"More likely we'll run into Germans," Dexter replied, opening the chamber of his submachine gun and looking inside.

"Well," said Doyle, "I still think we ought to split up. Why don't you two go together, and Sergeant Jones and I will go together. I think two will be better than one alone, because one can always cover the other if there's any trouble. Also, two will be less conspicuous than four."

Mazursky cleared his throat. "You're awfully conspicuous as it is in that officer's hat, sir."

"I'll have to get some German clothes from someplace, and so will all of us except you, Mazursky. It's not going to be a picnic no matter how you look at it, but I'd rather be on the loose than in those cells. At least this way we've all got a fighting chance. Okay, let's not waste any more time. Sergeant Jones and I will go in a westerly direction slightly to the south, and you two will go westerly slightly to the north. Good luck, and I hope we meet again someday."

They all shook hands, and then Lieutenant Doyle and Sergeant Okie Jones left in their designated direction through the forest, and after a few minutes, Mazursky and Dexter trudged in their direction.

The forest was eerie in the moonlight and glistening snow. Mazursky and Dexter waded through the branches, their breaths making puffs of smoke. They were hungry and cold, but at least they were free for the time being.

"I think we ought to keep moving at night and rest during the day," Mazursky said.

"Yeah, that's what I was thinking. We should put as much distance between us and that truck as possible."

They continued to make their way through the forest. They crossed frozen swamps, climbed hills, and descended into valleys. To slake their thirst they ate handfuls of snow. They saw lacelike clouds float across the half moon that hung in the sky, and they heard the hooves of deer that they startled.

At 0100 hours in the morning they stopped to rest in a cedar forest. Sitting on their haunches at the base of some trees, they looked around them and saw that bark recently had been eaten off some of the trees, and on the ground there were little piles of deer shit.

"Looks like deer come here," Dexter said. "Wish I could get my hands on one of them. Deer make damn fine eating."

"I wouldn't know. I never ate one," Mazursky replied.

"You fucking city slickers don't know what's good."

"Shut your rap, will you?"

"We got to get something to eat pretty soon. I can't go on like this."

"That's what you think."

"This is country, and there must be a farmhouse around someplace. Maybe we ought to climb a tree in the morning and see if we can find a farmhouse. That way maybe we can get some chickens and eggs."

"We also might get bullets in our ass. I think it's best that we stay out of sight."

"If we don't get something to eat pretty soon, we're going to starve to death."

"Shut the fuck up, will you Dexter? You're giving me a pain in my ass."

Mazursky and Dexter weren't the only creatures anxious about food in that Cedar forest. In the tree above them was a wild cat similar to the bobcats found in the forests of North America. This cat came to that cedar forest because he knew deer also went there to feed on the cedar bark. He'd already killed seven deer there and tonight was looking for number eight. Instead there were two small creatures down there, and they weren't eating bark. They were making strange sounds. The cat could sense that they were good to eat. Licking his chops, he poised himself to strike.

"How far do you think our lines are?" Dexter asked.

"About a hundred miles, I'd estimate. We'll know when we get close, because we'll hear the shellfire."

"I don't know how we'll get through."

"It won't be easy."

"They'll shoot you if you leave that German uniform on. You'll have to take it off."

"They're liable to shoot us anyway, because we won't know the password."

"So what are we trying to get back for?"

"Because it's our only chance."

DOOM PLATOON

At that moment the cat dropped down from his branch. Silently he passed through the air, his claws outstretched. He landed on Mazursky, sank his claws, and took a bite of Mazursky's closest available surface, which happened to be the German helmet he was wearing. The cat's teeth ground against the steel, Mazursky was paralyzed with pain and terror, and Dexter, recovering quickly, whacked the cat in the head with the butt of his submachine gun. Dazed, the cat tried to bite again, and bent his teeth once more. Dexter swung harder this time and caught the cat's head between his rifle butt and Mazursky's helmet. The cat went unconscious and Dexter pulled him off Mazursky. The cat dropped to the ground and Dexter beat his head in with the rifle butt, then turned to Mazursky who was bleeding from holes in his German uniform.

"Are you okay?" Dexter asked.

"That fucking no good cat!"

"Did he hurt you?"

"I don't know."

"If you can talk like that, I guess he didn't hurt you. Let me take a look."

Dexter inspected the holes in Mazursky' s uniform. He wasn't bleeding too badly. The thick layers of clothing prevented the claws from going in too deeply. Mazursky stood up, and made fists.

"Where's that fucking cat?" he said, looking at the ground. "I'm going to stomp that son of a bitch into the ground!"

Dexter pushed Mazursky away from the cat. "Calm down you stupid prick."

"Lemme at that cat!"

"Keep your fucking hands off him!"

"I'm not going to touch him with my hands! I'm going to kick his fucking ass!"

"Oh no you're not."

"Why not?"

"Because he's my supper."

"Supper?"

"That's right, you birdbrain. That cat is made out of meat, and meat is food."

Mazursky looked at the cat in a new light. "Hey, that's right."

"You're damn right it's right." Dexter kneeled beside the cat. "If only I had a knife."

"I think there's a knife in one of these pockets," Mazursky said, searching through the German uniform he was wearing. "Here it is." He handed it to Dexter.

Dexter opened the blade and ran his thumb over the edge. "Pretty sharp," he said. He bent over the cat, stabbed the knife into the top of its stomach, and ripped down. Dark blood welled out of the deep gash. "Want a drink of blood?"

"Do you think I'm a fucking vampire?"

"Then I guess you won't mind if I have some." Dexter lowered his face to the gash, put his mouth against it, and drank the cat's warm blood.

Mazursky looked at him with a mask of horror and distaste on his face. "I've never seen anything so disgusting in all my life."

"Tastes good," Dexter said, gulping down blood.

"I think I'm going to throw up."

"And it's good for me, too. Are you sure you don't want some."

"I'm not that hungry."

"In a few days you'll be hungry enough to eat the ass end out of a skunk. In the mean time, do you think you'd like a little of this fine raw cat meat?"

"I think I'll try some. Can you cut anything like a steak out of it?"

"Hey, this ain't no fucking cow."

"I can see it ain't no fucking cow."

"I can give you a chunk of its ass."

"A chunk of its ass? I ain't eating no cat's ass."

"How about a shoulder?"

"Isn't there a regular piece of meat that you can slice off?"

"I think I can cut you something."

Dexter cut into the cat's leg in three places, got a grip on its skin, and pulled it away. This left a length of bare flesh on its haunch uncovered. He sliced off a strip of meat and handed it to Mazursky. "Here."

Mazursky took it with the tips of his fingers and wrinkled his nose. "Looks awful."

Dexter was cutting off a piece for himself. "Eat it and shut up."

Mazursky raised the meat to his nose. It had no smell at all. He bit into it, and it was gristly and slimy. He spit out the blood and juice that had got in his mouth.

"What's the matter with you?" Dexter asked.

"I can't eat this stuff," Mazursky said, laying his piece of meat on the incision that Dexter had made.

"I can." Dexter raised his piece to his lips and took a bite. He rolled his eyes in ecstasy. "It tastes real good. Almost as good as possum." Then he chewed and swallowed.

"Dexter, anybody who'd eat that would eat shit."

"Starve to death, see if I care."

"As far as I'm concerned, that's not food."

"So starve to death."

Mazursky ate a handful of snow. It filled him up a little. He ate another handful. It filled him up more. Dexter finished his piece of meat and then started on Mazursky's.

"It's delicious," Dexter said, chewing happily. "If you had this in a New York restaurant it'd cost you fifty dollars a plate."

"That don't serve shit like that in New York restaurants. They don't even put shit like that in hot dogs." He took another handful of snow. His mouth still tasted horrible from the cat meat.

"In a few days you're going to wish you had some of this."

"Bullshit. I'm going to find me some real food."

"This is real food."

"That's shit food. Mazursky don't eat shit food."

"Where are you going to get real food?"

"I'll find some—don't worry about it."

"I think you're going to starve to death. If you do, I'm not going to take the trouble to bury you. I'll just leave you for his cousin." He pointed his thumb at the cat.

"Mazursky will never starve to death. Mazursky is going to have a good hot meal tomorrow."

"Where?"

"I don't know yet."

"Maybe you can hitch a ride into Berlin and have dinner with Hitler."

"Maybe you can go fuck yourself."

Dexter cut off another piece of meat and took a bite. Then he spat violently. "A little fur was on that piece."

"I'm surprised you didn't swallow it anyways, you scumbag."

Dexter cut another piece and carefully trimmed off the fur.

"I wonder how that Air Corps officer and the hillbilly are doing?" Mazursky asked, chewing another handful of Snow.

"They're probably doing about as good as we're doing."

"I can't wait to get back to my outfit. We had a good mess sergeant."

"I didn't. I don't think he knew a piece of bacon from a string bean."

"You know what I could go for right now, Dexter? A big bowl of beef stew, with bread just the way my mother used to bake it, and lots of butter, and a bottle of Knickerbocker beer."

"They say that when guys are starving to death they start talking about food that way. I think you're starting to starve to death. Are you sure you don't want some of this delicious cat."

"Shove it up your ass."

"I wish there was some way to bring with us what we don't eat."

"That's your problem. I told you that I'm going to have a good hot meal tomorrow."

"Sure. And a bottle of Knickerbocker beer."

"I know you don't believe me, but I'll show you."

"Sure you will."

Dexter leaned back and stuck a dirty fingernail into his teeth, picked out a piece of gristle, put it on his tongue, and swallowed it. "Well, that's enough for now," he said. "Don't want to make a pig of myself. Don't want to get sick." He took a handful of snow to wash down his meal. "I feel like a new man."

"You're disgusting, Dexter. All you guys in the tank corps are animals. Everybody knows that."

Dexter looked at him and raised his eyebrows. "Who said I'm in the tank corps?"

"Didn't you say you were in the 7th Cav?"

"Yeah, but that wasn't my regular unit. You see, I was wounded in my regular unit, and when I got out of the hospital, they put me as a replacement in the 7th Cav, because they were on the front lines then and taking a shellacking. I was one of the tank support troops when I got taken prisoner."

"What was your regular outfit."

Dexter puffed out his chest. "The 53rd Airborne Division."

"What!"

"That's right," Dexter said proudly.

"You're a fucking paratrooper?"

"All the way," replied Dexter.

"I knew there was some reason why you were all fucked up, and now I know. You're a goddamn asshole paratrooper."

"What are you, Mazursky? Just another dogface

infantry soldier?"

"Your goddamned right! And proud of it!"

"How can anybody be proud to be in the infantry when any damn nitwit who can walk and pull a trigger gets put into the infantry?"

"How can anybody with any brains want to jump out of airplanes?"

"You're just jealous."

"Jealous of what? Of being crazy?"

"We're the elite troops and you're just jealous."

"Elite troops! Are you fucking kidding?"

"They always send the paratroopers to the toughest spots because we're the best."

"And then the infantry has to come and bail you out. The paratroopers are a joke, for crying out loud. The Germans shot you right out of the air in Normandy. I should have known that anybody who'd eat a cat would also jump out of an airplane."

"You ugly dogface son of a bitch!"

"You sissy paratrooper cocksucker!"

They sat in the snow glaring at each other through the darkness. Then Mazursky perked up his ears.

"I hear something," he said.

"I hear it too."

It was a faint droning sound coming from far away in the east. They sat and listened, and the sound grew louder.

"It's our Air Corps," Dexter said, a smile on his face.

"Too bad you couldn't be up in one of those planes, so you could jump out."

"If I did, I'd hope I'd land feet first on your big fat

head."

Then came the rumbling of anti-aircraft fire. Lights flashed on the horizon. The droning became louder and then they saw the planes coming like an immense swarm of locusts against the night sky. Mazursky and Dexter stood and look up as the air armada passed overhead.

"I bet that air field takes another pounding tonight," Mazursky said.

"I think all of Germany's gonna take a pounding tonight."

The planes passed out of sight on the horizon, and the droning sound became fainter. Then the rumbling of exploding bombs could be heard, and the horizon to the east flashed and flickered.

Dexter picked up his submachine gun. "I think we'd better get going."

Mazursky grunted assent, and they started walking toward the west, where the planes had come from. They climbed a hill, came down the other side, and were in a thick pine forest when Dexter stopped suddenly.

"I don't feel so good," he said.

"What's the matter."

"I think I'm going to throw up."

"Oh, you fucking asshole."

Mazursky walked away and looked toward the east, where he could hear the sounds of the planes getting louder again. Behind him he could hear Dexter retching. He turned around. "What's the matter, Dexter? Cat meat don't agree with you?"

Dexter clutched his guts and puked the reddish gunk

onto the snow. Tears ran down his cheeks and his whole body shivered in the moonlight. Mazursky looked away and shook his head. "Fucking asshole," he muttered.

Dexter had the dry heaves for a while, and he leaned against a tree, feeling weak and dizzy. "I think I'll have to lie down for awhile," he said.

"I told you not to eat that cat."

"I thought it was a good idea to eat some meat."

"Yeah, but you're a paratrooper. You don't know how to think and you shouldn't try."

"Give me a break, will you Mazursky?"

"Of all the guys to team up with, I had to team up with you. A fucking paratrooper who likes to eat cats."

"Don't say that word again. It'll make me throw up."

"What word? You mean *cat?*"

Dexter went into the dry heaves again. "You bastard," he moaned, drooling onto the snow.

"Okay, I won't say *cat* anymore."

Dexter kept dry heaving, then he sat at the base of a tree and leaned against the trunk. "I think I'm going to die," he said.

"Anybody who eats a raw cat deserves to die."

"Maybe we'd better stop here for the night."

"You're slowing me down, paratrooper."

"Then maybe you'd better go on without me."

"Naw, I'll stick with you. I don't think you could make it alone."

"You cocksucker."

"What did that cat taste like anyway?"

Dexter started dry heaving again. Mazursky cleared

away the snow at the base of a tree and sat down. He was happy for the opportunity to take a rest, for he was fatigued and weak from hunger, but he didn't want Dexter to think that he *needed* a rest, because he wanted to out-macho Dexter, since Dexter was a hated paratrooper.

After a while Dexter stopped dry heaving. He washed his face and growth of beard with snow, ate some to clean out his mouth, and then cleared away some snow underneath a spruce tree, lay down, and closed his eyes. Despite the cold, he fell asleep almost instantly.

Mazursky was too tired to clear away any more snow. He couldn't even bring himself to move. Hugging himself with his arms for additional warmth, he closed his eyes and soon was asleep.

Chapter Nine

THE PERCUSSIVE SOUND of axe against tree echoed through the woods. Mazursky opened his eyes. It was a sunny morning. He looked at his watch; it was 0830 hours. The sound of the axe didn't appear too far away. He felt floaty from lack of food and there was a cramp in his empty stomach.

"You up, Mazursky?" Dexter asked, lying in the snow and looking at him with baleful eyes.

"You can see, can't you?"

"It sounds like somebody's chopping down a tree."

"I know. Maybe whoever it is has some food with him. Let's go find out."

Both men got up, brushed snow off themselves, and ate some snow for breakfast. Dexter worked the bolt of his submachine gun, took out the clip of ammunition, and replaced it.

"I'm ready to go," Dexter said.

"It sounds like it's coming from over there." Mazursky pointed.

171

They walked through the woods toward the sound, pushing branches out of their way, breathing hard from their slight exertions. Mazursky saw spots before his eyes and his legs felt like rubber. His stomach felt like the Grand Canyon.

"How're you feeling this morning?" he asked Dexter.

"Much better," Dexter lied. "How about you?"

"Terrific."

"You look like death warmed over."

"So do you, you paratrooper bastard."

They made their way through the woods, and the chopping grew louder. Then through the branches and underbrush they saw two figures and a horse. One of the figures was wielding the axe and chopping down a spruce tree about eight feet high. Mazursky and Dexter crouched behind a bush and watched.

"I think we should rush them," Mazursky said.

"I think you're right. Maybe we should creep a little closer, so we won't have to run so far."

"Good idea, and don't fire unless you have to; we don't want to attract any attention."

They crept around the bush and moved toward the two figures and the horse in the clearing. They were on their stomachs, gulping for air, nearly fainting, both nearly white as the snow, their eyes sunken into their heads. The spruce tree fell down, and the two figures proceeded to affix it to a harness that trailed behind the horse.

Suddenly Mazursky and Dexter stopped, their eyes goggling.

"They're women!" Mazursky hissed between his teeth.

Dexter's jaw dropped open, for they were indeed

women wearing long woolen dresses and thick mackinaws, with babushkas on their heads and boots on their feet.

"Pussy," Dexter whispered.

"They're getting ready to go. We'd better make our move now."

"Okay, let's go."

"Up and at 'em!"

The two weakened and woozy sergeants came up from behind the bush and charged the two women in the clearing, who first looked at them in surprise, and then terror as they saw the submachine gun in Dexter's hand. Their faces drained of color, they looked at each other fearfully, and began to tremble. They were around forty years old, and they held each other's hands as Mazursky and Dexter stopped in front of them.

One of the women said something in German; it sounded as though she were begging.

Mazursky looked at Dexter. "You know how to say food in German?"

Dexter shook his head. "I can't say a fucking word in German."

One of the women attempted to smile. "You are Americans?" she asked in German-accented English.

"Yes," said Mazursky and Dexter in unison, astonished.

"You are soldiers?"

"Yes."

The woman looked at the other woman. "I had no idea the Americans were this close."

The other woman shrugged. "You never know what to believe these days," she said in accented English.

"The Americans aren't this close," Mazursky said. "We've escaped from the prisoner of war camp in Schwanditz. How come both of you speak English?"

"We both studied English at the University of Heidelberg. May we introduce ourselves?"

"Go ahead."

"I am the Baroness Helga Von Kanzow, and this is my cousin, the Countess Lilli von Bitburg."

Mazursky and Dexter looked them over. The Baroness had blue eyes and thin lips, while the Countess had brown eyes and more sensuous lips. They didn't look too bad, particularly after six months on the front lines.

"I am Sergeant Michael Mazursky of the 25th United States Infantry Regiment," Mazursky said, removing his helmet and bowing slightly, which he felt was appropriate in the presence of royalty.

"I am Sergeant Bull Moose Dexter of 125th Airborne," Dexter added. "Do you have any food with you by any chance?"

'Food?" said the Baroness, who was somewhat taller than the Countess. "We don't have any with us, but we have some back at the manor. Are you hungry?"

"Are you kidding?" asked Dexter.

"Who else lives back at the manor?" Mazursky asked.

"No one. We live alone."

"Then where is the Baron and the Count?"

"They are on the Eastern Front, and all our servants have been conscripted into the Army. My cousin and I are all alone."

Dexter brandished his submachine gun. "Lady, we're

desperate men. The SS is looking for us right now. If you're lying, I'll kill you without even thinking about it."

The Baroness looked insulted. "Why should I lie to you?"

"Because you're Germans, and we're Americans, and our countries are at war."

"I have signed no declaration of war. I am not mad at anybody," said the Baroness.

"Nor am I," said the Countess.

"This was has been a terrible inconvenience for us," said the Baroness. "That Adolf Hitler is a little Austrian madman and I can't understand how he ever got as far as he did."

"This is the first Christmas in my life," the Countess said, "where there have been no men around to chop down our Christmas tree."

Mazursky and Dexter looked at each other.

"This is Christmas?" Mazursky asked.

The Baroness shook her head. "Tomorrow is Christmas. Tonight is Christmas Eve. We must put the tree up tonight. Would you be so kind as to help us?"

"Sure," said Dexter, "if you would be so kind as to feed us."

The Baroness raised her nose in the air. "We do not let guests go hungry, Sergeant, although I'm afraid our cuisine is not as distinguished as it has been in the past."

Dexter jiggled his submachine gun again. "It wouldn't be very healthy for you ladies if you tried to fool us, or betray us to the SS."

She raised her eyebrows. "The SS? Those homosexuals

and sadists? People like my cousin and myself don't have anything to do with people like that."

"I should say not!" the Countess added emphatically. "The very idea!"

"They have no dignity, no breeding."

"They are scum."

"The lowest of the low."

"A conglomeration of sex perverts."

Mazursky finished hitching up the Christmas tree to the harness, they began to move through the forest. Mazursky and Dexter were suspicious, ready to fight and run at any moment. But they were willing to take chances, because they were close to starvation.

The Baroness was talking to the Countess. "I rather like the idea of entertaining these Americans," she said. "It reminds me of stories I heard about the First World War, when our pilots would entertain enemy pilots they'd shot down, and vice versa. That was the last war where there was any sense of chivalry."

"Yes," said the Countess, "war used to be the domain of gentlemen, but now everybody is being positively beastly."

They came to the edge of the woods, and stretching below was a meadow and the manor house, a three-story stone building in the shape of a crescent. Farm buildings were nearby, as were landscaped trees. A driveway in front of the house led away through woods.

"How far away is the main road?" Mazursky asked.

"Two miles," said the Baroness.

"You're sort of isolated from the world here."

"No one ever comes here. It gets rather lonely at times.

It will be a pleasure to entertain you gentlemen."

"That's very kind of you to say, ma'am, but Dexter and me aren't gentlemen. We're just ordinary soldiers."

"You both are noble fighting men, true warriors, gladiators if you will. Such men as you are gentlemen regardless of where you were born, for you have distinguished yourselves on the field of battle."

"How do you know that?"

"Only extraordinary men could have escaped from a prisoner of war camp, and besides, a callous type of human being would have killed my cousin and me just because we were Germans, but you didn't. You took pity on us because we were women. You had the depth of soul to see that people like you and people like me are above the stupidity of this war."

They walked down the meadow to the barn, Dexter leading the horse by its harness and talking to the Countess, who laughed with a lilting soprano voice at his jokes. In the barn, they hitched the horse in his stall. In the next stall mooed a cow, and all the other stalls were empty.

"The Army took away our other cows," said the Baroness. "They only left us this one, and some chickens and pigs. If the war isn't over soon, we won't have anything to eat."

"It'll be over soon," Mazursky said. "The Allies will be here before long."

"I certainly hope so. Now if you gentlemen will carry the tree, we'll go to the manor and get something to eat."

Mazursky picked up the trunk and Dexter took the top of the tree. It wasn't a very big tree, but they were pretty weak by this time, and they stumbled behind the baroness and countess as they led the way across the back yard to the rear door of the manor.

They found themselves, in an enormous kitchen with a large black cast iron stove and a table with a bench on either side.

"We spend most of our time in the kitchen because we try to conserve fuel," the Baroness said, removing her babushka and revealing golden hair that fell to her shoulders.

The Countess looked at her. "But now that we have gentlemen guests, perhaps we can have our dinner meal in the dining room." The Countess removed her babushka, and she had wavy brunette hair that gleamed in the sunlight streaming through the large windows.

"I think that's a marvelous idea," said the Baroness.

The ladies removed their mackinaws and hung them near the door. Underneath they wore blouses that showed well-developed bosoms. Mazursky and Dexter would have gotten horny were they not so hungry.

"They look awfully hungry," said the Countess. "What should we feed them?"

"I don't know." The Baroness looked at the two bleary-eyed soldiers. "What would you like, gentlemen?"

"Whatever is fastest," Mazursky replied immediately.

"Oh dear me they must be starving," said the Baroness. "Why don't you give them some bread, while I slice some ham."

The Countess opened the breadbox, took out a loaf of bread, unwrapped it, and placed it before Mazursky and

Dexter, who started tearing it apart and stuffing it into their mouths before she could get the butter. Plates and silverware were placed on the table, along with a huge ham, a pitcher of milk, and some cold potatoes that had been boiled the night before.

"I'd warm all this up for you, gentlemen, but I don't think you'd want to wait," said the Baroness.

"We wouldn't," said Mazursky through a mouth full of ham, bread, potatoes, and milk.

Gradually their hunger subsided, and they were able to eat more leisurely. The ladies made coffee and sat with them.

"This tastes like real coffee," Dexter said, sipping from a cup made of fine china.

"It is," the Baroness said proudly. "My husband filled the larder with many items he thought would get scarce, and then he left for war."

"When did you see him last?"

"Last Easter he got a furlough."

"It's been almost a year, then."

The Baroness looked sad. "Yes."

"What does he do in the Army?"

"He is a Colonel on the staff of General Von Katoffle."

"My husband," said Lilli, "is a colonel in the Quartermaster Corps. I haven't seen him since Easter either."

Dexter chortled. "I wonder what they'd both think if they saw you here having coffee with a couple of American soldiers."

The Baroness smiled. "I'm sure they'd join you and offer you cigars."

"Cigars?" asked Mazursky. "You have cigars?"

"Certainly. My husband always keeps a private stock of cigars in the house. Would you like one?"

"That'd be terrific."

"Excuse me," she said, getting up from the bench and walking out of the kitchen.

Mazursky ate another piece of ham and wondered if she was calling the SS. Dexter looked at him suspiciously, evidently thinking the same thing. She returned a few minutes later with a mahogany cigar humidor. Setting it on the table, she opened the lid. Inside were claro and maduro cigars of various shapes.

"Help yourselves, gentlemen," the Baroness said.

Mazursky selected a black nasty-looking cigar that had the shape of a football. He put it in his mouth and lit it with his trusty old Zippo. The smoke filled his mouth with rich heady aroma. He leaned back and puffed away, reflecting on the peculiar ups and downs that a human life could take. He also reflected that the Baroness and Countess were good-looking old broads. Dexter likewise was puffing a cigar, wondering how he could get into the Countess's pants.

"Is there anything else you gentlemen would like?" the Countess asked pleasantly.

Dexter was about to ask her to sit on his face, but Mazursky spoke first.

"Could we possibly take a bath?" Mazursky asked.

"Why of course," the Baroness said. "Come with me, please."

Everyone stood up. Dexter picked up his submachine gun.

"Surely you're not going to take that thing with you wherever you go," the Baroness said chidingly.

"I never go anyplace without my gun, ma'am."

"Well," Mazursky said, "we never know when the SS might show up."

"They wouldn't dare come here."

"I don't feel safe unless I got my gun with me, ma'am," Dexter said. "I hope you won't mind."

"Well, if you must."

The ladies led them through a series of rooms and corridors decorated with paintings and the heads of wild game. The furniture was old and plush. On some walls were crossed swords and spears.

"This manor is very old," the Baroness said. "It has been in my husband's family for more than three hundred years. Bismarck himself slept here, as have many of Germany's leading personages."

"You don't say," Mazursky said, feeling like a shithouse rat in these elegant surroundings.

They climbed a curving hand-carved staircase and came to a carpeted corridor.

"I imagine each of you gentlemen would prefer a room of your own," the Baroness said.

"Naturally," said Dexter.

"I thought so. Lilli, why don't you take Sergeant Dexter to the Green Room, and I'll take Sergeant Mazursky to the Yellow Room."

Both couples separated in the corridor, Countess Lilli and Dexter going to the right, and Baroness Helga and Mazursky going to the left.

The Baroness opened a door on the corridor, and Mazursky stepped inside. The walls were yellow, the drapes were yellow, and the bedspread was yellow. On one of the walls was an oil painting of a man in a strange military uniform astride a horse.

"This will be your room," the Baroness said. "Do you like it?"

"It's very nice. Who's the guy in the picture?"

"That is the great-uncle of my husband, Prince Max Von Sperling. The bathroom is this way."

She led him across the bedroom to a door, opened it, and showed him the large bathroom and its luxurious porcelain fixtures.

"Where does your hot water come from?" Mazursky asked.

"We have a coal furnace in the cellar."

"Who shovels the coal?"

She smiled. "Who do you think?"

"That's no job for women."

"But there are no men here to help us."

"There are now."

She looked him up and down. "I know."

Then she looked away. "You'll find a razor in this cabinet here, and towels in that cabinet there. I'll get some of my husband's clothes and lay them on the bed outside. You're taller than he, and he's a little thicker around the waist, but I think they'll be all right. Now I'll leave you alone, because I'm sure you're anxious to get cleaned up."

"Thank you so much for everything, Baroness Helga."

Her blue eyes twinkled. "It is my pleasure, Sergeant Mazursky."

DOOM PLATOON

She left the bathroom and closed the door behind her. Mazursky, still puffing the cigar, stripped off his filthy stinking clothes and threw them in a corner. It was the first time in weeks that he'd seen himself naked, and was surprised by how much weight he'd lost. But his shoulders were still broad, and his muscles still hard. It was just the excess weight that'd gone away.

He went to the sink, turned on the water, took the safety razor, shaving brush, and soap bowl out of the cabinet, and shaved. It was rough going because he hadn't shaved for awhile, and he nicked himself a few times. But slowly his swarthy, ruggedly handsome features emerged. He smiled at himself. "Hi Mazursky," he said.

There was a new toothbrush wrapped in cellophane in the cabinet, and some tooth powder. He brushed his teeth and felt refreshed by the taste, for his mouth had been tasting foul for so long. Then he filled the bathtub with hot water, while puffing the remainder of the cigar, and when it was filled he put the cigar on an ashtray beside the sink, and got into the tub.

The water stung those places where the cat had clawed him, but he gritted his teeth and washed them. When the caked blood and dirt was gone he could see that the wounds were just shallow cuts and were healing well. Looking down to his right thigh, he saw the stitch marks on the wound he'd received on Omaha Beach. It hardly ever bothered him anymore. Taking the wash cloth and soap, he cleaned himself thoroughly, scrubbing away the layers of dirt. Then he rinsed off, drained the water out of the tub, and filled it again with fresh water. He lit the cigar stub, lay in the water, and closed his eyes, puffing away. If you're good, all good things will come to you, he thought. That's what his mother used to say.

There was a knock on the bathroom door. "Are you all right, Sergeant Mazursky?" the Baroness asked.

"Yes ma'am."

"I can't hear you. May I open the door?"

"Go ahead."

She opened the door and was surprised to see a handsome broad-shouldered man lying in the bathtub smiling at her, the end of a cigar in his straight white teeth. The sight of him took her breath away.

"Perhaps I should come in and shut the door," she said. "I wouldn't want you to get a draft."

"Good idea."

She entered the bathroom and closed the door behind her, leaning her hands back against it. "My, what a handsome man you are, Sergeant."

"I look a lot different when I'm all cleaned up, I guess."

She looked at his straight black hair that glistened in the sunlight coming in through the window. "I should say so. You look like a Greek god."

"I'm not Greek. I'm Polish."

"Then you look like a Polish god."

"You look pretty nice yourself, ma'am."

"Is everything all right?"

"Yes ma'am, everything's fine."

"I was wondering if you wanted chicken or roast pork for supper tonight."

"Either one's okay with me."

"But don't you have a preference?"

"Chicken, I guess."

"Very well. Chicken it will be. I've put some clothing on the bed for you. I think you'll like them."

"Anything will be better that what I've been wearing," he said nervously.

She wondered what he was so nervous about, and then she saw his penis break through the water in the bathtub. He was getting an erection. She hadn't seen a man's erection since her husband was on furlough last Easter. That had been almost a year ago.

"Would you like me to scrub your back, Sergeant Mazursky?" she asked.

"Oh, you don't have to, ma'am."

"That's all right. I don't mind."

"If you don't mind, that would be awfully nice. I can't reach back there too well."

"Turn around in the tub and lean forward."

"Yes ma'am."

He got up and turned his back to her, and in that brief moment she saw his muscular haunches, and wanted to grab them. Instead she soaped up the wash cloth and scrubbed his back.

"I thought Polish people had blond hair," she said, running the washcloth over his back.

"My mother was Italian."

"What an interesting combination."

"The best part of it was that I got to eat two different kinds of food all the time."

"I hope you like German cooking."

"I like all kinds of cooking, so long as it's good cooking."

"I hope my cooking will come up to your high standards."

"Don't worry about it. My standards aren't so high anymore."

She let the wash cloth drop, and ran her hands over his shoulders. "What did you do before you were drafted into the Army?"

"I wasn't drafted. I joined up."

"What did you do in civilian life?"

"I worked in a clothes factory, and then I was laid off. After that I joined the Army. There was a Depression in my country, you know."

"There was one here too."

She squeezed his shoulders and thought that if it weren't for the war she'd never dream of being alone with a man like this from a social class so obviously beneath her. But she was lonely, anxious, and horny. We must eat, drink, and be merry, for tomorrow we all might die, she thought. A stray bomb might fall on the manor and that might be the end of everything.

"I'm going to do something very naughty, Sergeant," she said. "I hope you won't get too upset."

"Do whatever you like, ma'am. It's your house."

She reached around His waist, grabbed his cock, and squeezed it, kissing his neck. "Oh Sergeant," she moaned.

He took her hand off his cock, and she realized that she had committed a terrible *faux pas,* that he wasn't attracted to her, probably he thought her too old and ugly.

"I'm so sorry," she said stammering, standing up. "I didn't mean to take advantage of the situation."

He stood, turned around, and stepped out of the bathtub, his cock sticking out like a lance. She realized it was bigger than the Baron's.

"Don't apologize," he said with a smile. "Everything's gonna be okay."

He took her in his arms and fastened his mouth on hers. She hugged his wet warm body and nearly fainted with ecstasy. He cupped her ass in his hands and pressed her crotch against him. She swiveled her hips so she could feel it better.

"Let's go to bed," he whispered into her ear.

"Yes."

He opened the door and led her into the bedroom. Sunlight bounced off the yellow walls and made everything golden. He took the clothes off the bed and placed them on a chair as she unbuttoned her blouse with trembling hands. She took the blouse off, reached behind her, and unhooked the brassiere. It fell away, showing her soft round breasts and hard pointy nipples.

She unbuttoned her skirt but before she could finish he came at her, hugged her, and enclosed her left nipple with his mouth. She groaned and pulled his damp head tighter against her. He sucked it hard; it was the first tit he'd seen since he left England more than six months ago.

He picked her up and placed her on the bed. Then he unbuttoned her skirt and pulled it away along with her petticoats, stockings, and boots. Now she lay only in white lace underpants that she'd bought in Paris in 1938. He inserted his fingers into the waistband and drew them down slowly, uncovering the fleecy blonde hair at the juncture of her legs. Blood pounding in his ears, he bent over and kissed the hair, and licked the moistening slit.

He pulled off her underpants and threw them over his shoulder. She spread her legs and he lowered himself between them, searching for her mouth with his tongue, hearing her moan and sigh. She took his cock in hand and stabbed it into her. He slid it in all the way, retreated, and then advanced again. She raised her legs in the air and wiggled her hips as he assaulted her most tender parts again and again.

Chapter Ten

AFTER THE BARONESS WENT DOWNSTAIRS, Mazursky

lay in bed for awhile, smoking a fresh cigar. He was pleased with the way things were turning out. He had an unlimited supply of cigars, food, and pussy, and no one was shooting at him. There was no reason to hurry back to the war. He deserved some rest and recuperation.

He got out of bed, stretched, and looked at the clothes the Baroness had brought him. He put on a pair of cotton boxer shorts and gray wool slacks that were a little big for him around the waist and a little short in the legs. The plaid shirt fit him nicely, as did the double-breasted blue blazer. There was a comb on the dresser, and he ran it through his thick black hair, parting it on the side. The black broughams were a good fit if he didn't lace them too tight.

There was a knock on the door.

"Come in."

Sergeant Bull Moose Dexter strolled into the room, attired in brown slacks and a green tweed sports jacket. He was smoking a cigarette, his curly sandy hair was combined straight back, and he looked a bit like Spencer Tracy now that he was shaved.

"How's it going?" Dexter asked nonchalantly, sitting on one of the chairs and crossing his legs.

"Pretty good. How about you?" Mazursky sat on one of the other chairs.

"Pretty good. You get any pussy yet?"

"Yeah. Did you?"

"Of course."

"How was it."

"Not bad. How was yours?"

"Pretty good."

Dexter blew a smoke ring into the air. "This is a pretty good set-up, ain't it?"

"Best duty I ever had."

"I was thinking that maybe we ought to rest here a little while and build up our strength."

"I was thinking the same thing. Besides, I don't know how we could make it through the German lines and into the Allied lines without getting killed."

"It'd be suicide to try."

"No point to it."

"None at all."

Mazursky puffed his cigar. "God damn, that woman knew how to move."

"The little countess gave me the best blow job of my life."

"They've got fine figures for old babes."

"Like young girls, for crying out loud!"

"There's just two problems," Mazursky said. "The first is that their husbands might come back, and the second is that the SS might come looking for us here."

"To hell with their husbands. We'll just bop them on the head if they give us any trouble. But you're right about the SS. We'd better bury our clothes and hide every trace that we're here."

"We've also got to find a hiding place for ourselves. Let's go down and talk to the ladies. They might know of one."

Mazursky and Dexter went downstairs, carrying their dirty clothing. The found the Baroness and Countess in the kitchen, preparing dinner. The aroma of cooking food was in the air, intermingled with expensive perfume.

"Ah, here are the gentlemen," said the Countess, looking up from the potato she was slicing.

The Baroness was tasting the soup in a pot. "Did you enjoy your baths, gentlemen?" she asked with a sly expression in her eyes.

"Oh yes, ma'am," said Mazursky.

"It was just what I needed," Dexter added.

The Baroness looked them up and down. "I can see that the clothes fit fairly well."

"Oh, they're very nice, ma'am," Mazursky said.

"The cat's pajamas," Dexter added.

"We thought," Mazursky said, "that we'd better hide our other clothes, in case the SS come here."

"They wouldn't dare come here," said the Baroness.

"Well, they might, and we ought to be prepared," Mazursky replied. "A couple of old soldiers like us know that anything can happen."

The Baroness shrugged. "I suppose you could bury them out in the barn, if you think it's necessary."

"We also think it's necessary that we have a place to hide ourselves."

"How about the cellar?"

"The cellar will be the first place they'll look."

"How about the attic?"

"That'll be the second place."

"How about a nice closet?""

"They'll look in all the closets, and under the beds, and in the barn. Is there any secret place in this house?"

The Baroness made a haughty face. "Secret place? There are no secret places in my home, sir. Why should there be?"

"For situations like this."

"But no situation like this has ever arisen before in the entire history of my family."

Mazursky looked at Dexter. "We'll have to search the place and see what we can find."

The Countess laid down her knife and wiped her hands on a cloth. "I think I know of a place where the gentlemen can hide."

"Where?" asked the Baroness.

"All of you come with me, and I'll show you."

She led them through a series of rooms and corridors to the huge living room, where a fire was burning in the fireplace. It had the usual paintings and animal heads on the walls, and suits of armor in the corners. It also had piano, a record player, and a radio.

"They can hide in here," the Countess said brightly.

"Where in here?" asked the Baroness.

"You can't think of any place where they can hide in here?"

The Baroness looked around. "None whatsoever."

"Neither can I," said Mazursky.

"Me neither," added Dexter.

The Countess smiled. "You see? The hiding place is so good, none of you are aware that it's here. Guess again."

The Baroness, Mazursky, and Dexter looked around the room.

"In the piano?" asked the Baroness.

"No, silly."

"Up the chimney?" asked Mazursky.

"That would be unbearably hot for you, Sergeant."

"You wouldn't have to light the fire."

"Then the room would get cold, and we wouldn't like to have a cold living room, would we?"

"I guess not."

The Countess looked at Dexter. "Where do you think you can hide, Sergeant Dexter?"

"How about underneath your dress?"

The Countess blushed. "You're being naughty."

"Sorry."

"Can't you think of a good hiding place in here?"

Dexter looked around the room again. "I can't see anything."

"Then I'll have to show you, won't I?" The pretty brunette Countess walked to one of the suits of armor and tapped the helmet. "In here."

"In there?" the Baroness asked, a bit bewildered.

"Certainly. Sergeant Mazursky and Sergeant Dexter will merely put on these suits of armor and stand still, if anybody comes looking for them. No one would ever dream that they're in the armor."

Mazursky smiled. "Hey, that's a pretty good idea."

The Countess fluttered her eyelashes. "I'm so glad you approve, Sergeant."

"Okay," Mazursky said, "If we're going to do this, we might as well do it right. Hereafter this house has to appear as though Baroness Helga and Countess Lilli are the only ones here. That means there can be no cigar butts in the ashtrays, or men's clothes lying around, or four beds being slept in. We've got to be ready for a search at a moment's notice. Does everybody understand that?"

The Baroness sniffed. "I think you're exaggerating, Sergeant. No one would dare search my home."

"We have to be prepared. It may be a matter of life and death."

"Well, if it'll make you happy we'll cooperate of course."

"Good." Mazursky looked at Dexter. "Let's go out to the barn and bury these clothes."

"Right."

"It's cold out there," Countess Lilli said. "Let me get your coats."

They went to the hall closet, and the Countess gave them men's mackinaws that had been worn by the Baron and the Count before the war. The women returned to their cooking in the kitchen, and the men went out to the barn.

Mazursky found a shovel near the barn door and they walked back, looking for a place to dig. But the floor was made of concrete.

"Hey," said Dexter. "Why don't we put it under the cow shit and horse shit? No one would ever dream of looking there."

Mazursky dug out some of the manure, and they dropped the clothing into the hole. Then Mazursky covered it up. They returned to the house, hung up their mackinaws, and sat in the living room near the fireplace, smoking cigars and cigarettes. A light snow began to fall, and the Baroness served them brandy, then returned to the kitchen.

"This is a fantastic set-up," Mazursky said. "I hope this fucking war goes on forever."

"I've never lived like this in my life," Dexter replied, his feet up on a cassock. "This brandy is smoother than honey."

"These cigars would cost a dollar apiece in New York."

"These old babes must have a lot of money."

"Yeah, I don't suppose they ever missed many meals, but if the war goes on for much longer, they're going to find out what it's like. The chickens and pigs can't hold out forever."

"How long you think the war will go on, Mazursky?"

"Who the fuck knows?"

"What are you going to do after it's over?"

"Shit, I don't know."

"You think you'll re-enlist?"

"I suppose that's what I'll wind up doing. The Army's all I know. How about you?"

"I'm going to try and buy some timberland up there in Maine, and go into the pulp business. Paper is made out of tree pulp, you know. There's a lot of money in it."

"You'd leave the Army?"

"You're fucking right I'd leave the Army."

"I always figured you weren't much of a soldier."

"I can out-soldier you any day of the week."

"Bullshit. You're just basically a civilian. It's assholes like you that join the paratroopers."

"You couldn't make it on the outside, Mazursky."

"Who in the fuck *wants* to make it on the outside? All you can do on the outside is get some kind of a boring stupid job for the rest of your life, or go into business like you want to and lose your ass. Even if you succeed in business, all that makes you is the head clerk. I'd rather be in the fucking Army."

"Only guys with no brains make a career out of the Army."

"Only guys who can't take Army life says things like that."

"I can take Army life, but I'm sick of it. I thought I was going to be a twenty year man, but enough is enough."

"Sissy."

"Idiot."

"Punk."

"Shithead."

They sat in front of the fireplace for the rest of the afternoon drinking brandy, arguing, and throwing logs on the fire. At around six o'clock in the evening Baroness Helga and Countess Lilli entered the living room, both wearing silk cocktail dresses. The Baroness's was white and the Countess's was black.

"Dinner is served, gentlemen," the Baroness said.

Mazursky and Dexter arose unsteadily, took their ladies' arms, and went to the dining room, which was aglow with candlelight and agleam with china and silver. The men seated themselves at the two ends of the table, while the women went into the kitchen for the first course, which was split pea soup in a silver tureen that had been in the Baroness's family for nearly four hundred years. The

Baroness carried the tureen while the Countess ladled it into bowls. Then the women sat at the table. They proceeded to dine.

"How do you like the soup?" the Baroness asked Mazursky.

"It's very good," he replied, trying to eat it without making the loud slurping noises he'd normally make in the mess hall.

"The best I ever had," Dexter added, holding the spoon daintily in his massive gnarled hand.

"Have you gentlemen been enjoying your day?" the Baroness asked.

"Yes ma'am," said Mazursky.

"Uh huh," added Dexter.

"That's good," she said, "because Countess Lilli and I thought you should have a day off, since you've both been through so much. But there's a lot of work to be done here and tomorrow you'll have to start helping us out. There are cows to be milked, animals to be fed, manure to be shoveled, wood to be chopped, coal to be shoveled, and so forth. Countess Lilli and I have been doing it all alone until now, and I don't have to tell you that we're not used to this type of work. Why, there were never less than ten servants on this estate in the old days. We hope you won't mind helping us."

Mazursky leaned forward and smiled. "Ladies, if you take care of the kitchen, Sergeant Dexter and myself will take care of everything else, won't we Sergeant Dexter?"

"Why sure, Sergeant Mazursky."

Baroness Helga looked at them through her sultry eyes. "That would be very kind of you, gentlemen."

"It's the least we could do, right Sergeant Dexter?"

"Right."

After the soup course, the main course was served. It consisted of a roast chicken, baked potatoes, and boiled carrots. A fine Riesling was poured by Countess Lilli.

"How do you keep all these vegetables fresh?" Mazursky asked.

"We keep them in the cellar," the Baroness replied. "Root vegetables keep that way for a long time. We have enough vegetables for about another year, but I don't think the meat will last until summer. I hope the war is over by then."

The dessert was baked applies, served with coffee. Then the women cleared off the table and washed the dishes, while the men sat before the fireplace, sipping brandy and smoking.

"What a fucking deal this is," Dexter said lazily.

"Pour me a little more brandy, will you Sergeant old boy?"

After a while the women returned to the living room.

"Do you know what we're going to do now?" Baroness Helga asked.

"What?" asked Mazursky.

"You mean you've forgotten?"

"Forgotten what?" asked Dexter.

"What night this is?"

"It's Christmas Eve!" Mazursky and Dexter said together.

"That's right, and we've got to decorate the tree."

The men went outside and got the tree, carrying it to the living room and setting it on the pedestal that the women brought down from the attic along with boxes of decorations. Together they decorated the tree, drank brandy, and sang Christmas carols. The men got so drunk that occasionally they forgot where they were and tried to cop cheap feels from the women, who slapped their hands. The Baroness put some records on the record player and they danced between the sofas and chairs, executing spins and sexy dips. They kissed and sighed. It was very romantic and lovey-dovey there in the light of the flickering fireplace.

Then a light flashed across the wall.

"What the fuck is that!" Mazursky said. He rushed to the window and peeked out the side of the curtains.

He saw four vehicles rolling over the driveway toward the house.

"I think it's a searching party," Mazursky said.

Countess Lilli looked out the window. "It's the SS," she said, turning pale.

"How do you know?" asked Dexter, who was looking out the side of another curtain.

"I can see the lightning bolt insignia on their license plate."

Mazursky and Dexter ran toward the suits of armor. They stepped into the iron pants, and the women helped them on with the iron jackets and helmets. Mazursky gripped the handle of the sword in his scabbard, while Dexter grabbed his spear. They both could see out the slits in their helmets.

The Baroness was furious. She paced back and forth gnashing her teeth. "How dare the SS come here!" she yelled. "Who do they think I am! If my husband were here he'd have them all shot!"

The caravan of black Mercedes-Benz limousines

stopped in front of the house, and black-uniformed SS men got out. They marched up to the front door and pounded on it.

"I'll handle them," Baroness Helga said, raising her chin in the air. She walked out of the living room, down the entrance hall, and opened the front door.

Standing before her was a troop of SS men. In front of them was a tall Captain with a long face and a few dueling scars on his cheeks. He had a nervous tic in one eye.

She gazed coldly at him. "What is the meaning of this interruption!"

He smiled obsequiously. "I'm terribly sorry to bother you madam, but several dangerous men have escaped from the prisoner of war camp at Schwanditz, and I would like to know if you have seen any strangers roaming about, by any chance."

"I have seen no one."

"Are you sure?"

"Quite sure."

"May I inquire who lives here?"

"You may not!"

The Baroness tried to slam the door in his face, but he stopped it with his hand.

"How dare you!" she screamed.

"Madam, I'm afraid you don't know who you're dealing with," he said.

"On the contrary sir, I don't think you know who *you're* dealing with!"

"I beg to differ with you. You are the Baroness Van Kanzow. And I am Captain Fritz Goertz of the SS." He reached into his pocket and took out a silver disc about two inches in diameter. It was embossed with a swastika and some words she couldn't read. "This is my warrant; it confers upon me unlimited rights of search, interrogation, arrest, and execution. We are going to search your buildings and grounds. Please get out of my way, or I'll have you shot."

"You wouldn't dare!"

He took out his Luger and pointed it at her head. "Don't tempt me. The decadent nobility like yourself have long stood in the way of The Fuehrer and his great plans for this country, but you shall not stand in my way here."

"You wouldn't dare shoot!" she shouted, puffing out her chest.

"Wouldn't I?" He flicked off the safety and took aim at her nose.

She realized he meant business, and stepped back. Captain Goertz ordered his men to search the house, surrounding buildings, and immediate area. They scurried off in all directions, their rifles and pistols at the ready. Some went into the manor, and Captain Goertz followed them. Then he stopped suddenly.

"Is that cigar smoke I smell?" he asked.

"I...well..." the Baroness stammered.

He charged down the hall and entered the living room, with the Baroness right behind him fearing the worst. They saw Countess Lilli sitting on the sofa, smoking Mazursky's cigar. She was a little green around the gills.

"Hello," she said with a faint smile. "Merry Christmas."

His mouth turned down at the corners. "Do you

customarily smoke cigars, madam?"

"All the time."

"How disgustingly decadent."

The Captain looked at the fireplace, the paintings, the Christmas tree, and the suits of armor.

Baroness Helga trembled with rage and indignation. "If my husband were here, you wouldn't dare invade my home this way."

Captain Goertz looked sideways at her and smirked. "If he spoke to me the way you have, madam, I'd take him to the nearest concentration camp and roast him alive."

"It's a disgrace that SS men like you are harassing good Germans while men like my husband are risking their lives on the Eastern Front."

He harrumphed. "The Eastern Front is collapsing because of men like your husband."

"Everyone knows that the worst scoundrels in Germany are in the SS," she countered.

"Don't try my patience, madam. Your life doesn't mean anything to me."

Countess Lilli was afraid the situation might get out of hand. She stood, smiled, and walked toward Captain Goertz.

"It's a pity, Captain, that you have to be out on Christmas Eve. I'm sure you'd much rather be with your family."

"That is correct, madam."

The Countess looked at the Baroness. "You should be more understanding, Helga. Where would the Reich be if it weren't for brave SS men like this Captain?"

"Better off."

Captain Goertz turned purple and reached for his

Luger again. Countess Lilli grabbed his wrist. "Don't let yourself be upset by a woman, sir. She can't help herself. You see, her husband tried to join the SS, and was rejected," Countess Lilli lied.

"Oh, so that's how it is?"

" Yes, Captain. It was a great blow to both of them, because they both wanted to be part of the SS. Now I'm afraid my cousin has grown bitter."

"I understand now," he said with a smile. "After all, not everyone can be accepted by our elite organization." The armor inhabited by Mazursky caught his eye. "That's a very interesting suit of armor. I think I'd like to take a closer look at it."

The Baroness and Countess tried to hide their consternation as Captain Goertz strode toward the suit of armor. The Countess was near collapse from the cigar she was smoking. Mazursky resolved to cleave Captain Goertz in twain if Goertz discovered him.

Captain Goertz touched the breastplate of the armor. "This is a very interesting piece. I believe it dates from the seventeenth century."

"An ancestor of my husband wore it in the War against the Turks in 1661," Baroness Helga said drily.

"You don't say."

"What was your family doing in 1661, Captain," the Baroness asked with a murderous edge in her voice.

"I haven't the slightest idea."

A sergeant marched into the living room, halted before Captain Goertz, and gave the Heil Hitler Salute. "We have conducted a thorough search, sir, and have found no one."

"You've looked everywhere?"

"Yes sir."

"Even in the cellar?"

"Yes sir."

"The attic?"

"Yes sir."

"Very well. Assemble your men and return to the vehicles."

"Yes sir."

The sergeant gave the Heil Hitler salute again, did an about-face, and left the room.

Captain Goertz tipped his hat and bowed slightly to the ladies. "That will be all. I'm so sorry to have inconvenienced you."

Baroness Helga glowered at him.

Countess Lilli stepped forward. "I'll see you to the door, sir."

"That would be very kind of you."

She led him out of the living room and through the corridor to the front door. He opened it, and the other SS men could be seen loading into the limousines.

"I'm sorry about the way my cousin behaved," the Countess said. "She's been quite distraught lately."

"You needn't apologize. These are difficult times for the Fatherland. Good night, madam."

"Good night, sir. And good luck with your search."

"Thank you."

Captain Goertz gave her a little salute, turned, and marched to his Mercedes-Benz, getting in behind the driver. The limousines were starting their engines as the

DOOM PLATOON

Countess closed the door. She returned to the living room. After the limousines had left the driveway, and their tail lights were tiny red dots in the distance, Mazursky and Dexter got out of their suits of armor, and the Christmas Eve celebration continued.

LEN LEVINSON

Chapter Eleven

IN THE DAYS THAT FOLLOWED, Mazursky and Dexter
went to the barn each morning to feed the animals, gather
the eggs, milk the cows, and shovel the shit, while the women
stayed in the house and did the cooking, house cleaning, and
laundry. They dressed for dinner each night, danced and
drank brandy in the living room, and went to bed. Toward the
end of January, Baroness Helga suggested they change bed
partners, citing variety as the spice of life, and everyone agreed.

The days grew longer, and soon it was March.
Mazursky and Dexter, during their hours in the barn, often
remarked on their idyllic existence, and expressed the desire
that it would go on forever. They confessed to each other
that they'd never been so happy in their lives. Their
temperaments improved to the point where they even
stopped insulting each other. Yet they knew that their
situation couldn't last forever.

The snow disappeared from the ground and buds burst
on the trees. The meadows turned pale green, and one day
a robin was seen on the lawn in front of the mansion. The

women were disconsolate after receiving letters from their husbands stating that the German Army was suffering heavy casualties in the East, but after a few days they regained their high spirits and switched partners again. One night, all four of them went to bed together.

On the second of April they heard the faint sound of artillery bombardments. The sounds were louder on the next day. Two days later they could hear machine gun and rifle fire. From the attic of the mansion they could see smoke on the horizon. On the next day they could see heavy troop movements heading toward the heartland of Germany on the road that was not far from the mansion.

"The German Army is retreating," Mazursky said.

"It looks like our vacation is just about over," Dexter replied glumly.

Mazursky turned to the Baroness and the Countess. "Will you miss us, girls?"

Tears filled the Baroness's eyes. "I shall never forget you."

"Nor shall I," added the Countess, reaching for her handkerchief.

It was decided that Mazursky and Dexter should go into hiding until the Germans were gone from the vicinity, because they could never tell when some German soldiers might visit the house. Thereafter Mazursky and Dexter always stayed in the house close to the suits of armor, but no Germans ever stopped in. They were too busy fleeing from the Allied Armies. Mazursky and Dexter drank lots of brandy and smoked lots of cigars, because they knew it was all coming to an end pretty soon. They also screwed the women every chance they had. The women seemed to enjoy the additional attention. But the atmosphere in the mansion became melancholy, because everyone knew that the dream bubble was about to burst.

Late one afternoon a long column of soldiers approached the mansion. Mazursky and Dexter ran to the suits of armor and commenced putting them on, when Baroness Helga, who was looking out the window, said, "They are not wearing German uniforms."

Mazursky and Dexter looked out the window, and sure enough, the soldiers were wearing the khaki uniforms of the United States Army. Mazursky and Dexter felt joy commingled with sorrow. On one hand they didn't have to worry anymore about being found by the SS, but on the other, they were going to be dogfaces again. The column of soldiers stopped in front of the house. Mazursky estimated that there were at least three companies out there. The soldiers looked filthy, bearded, and battle weary. There was a knock on the door.

Baroness Helga, Countess Lilli, Mazursky, and Dexter went to the front door. Baroness Helga opened it. Standing on the front porch was an American Lieutenant-Colonel and a few other officers. One of them made a statement in German.

Baroness Helga smiled. "We all speak English here," she said.

The Lieutenant-Colonel cleared his throat. "Madam, I'm afraid I must requisition your property for my battalion tonight. My officers will be staying in your house, and my men in the surrounding buildings. I apologize for the intrusion and any inconvenience we may be causing you, but we didn't start this war."

"I quite understand," she said graciously.

"I am Lieutenant-Colonel Matt Holmes," the officer said, bowing slightly," and these are two of my staff officers, Major Wooley and Captain Barnes."

"How do you do, Gentlemen. I am the Baroness Helga Von Kanzow, and this is the Countess Lilli Von Bitburg. The two men are Sergeant Michael Mazursky and Sergeant Bull Moose Dexter of your Army."

Mazursky and Dexter snapped to attention. The vacation was officially over.

Lieutenant-Colonel Holmes narrowed his eyes at them. "What are you two birds doing here?"

"We escaped from the POW camp at Schwanditz, sir," Mazursky said. "These ladies were kind enough to hide us from the SS. They risked their lives for us many times, sir, and we hope you'll mention that in your dispatches, sir."

"I see. Well, report to my quartermaster and get back into uniform immediately."

"Yes sir." Mazursky turned to the ladies. "Well, thanks for everything," he said.

"Yeah," added Dexter. "We couldn't have made it without you."

"It was a pleasure to help you," Baroness Helga said with a faint smile.

"We Germans are not as inhuman as people generally think," Countess Lilli added.

Baroness Helga turned to Lieutenant-Colonel Holmes. "May I show you my home; sir?"

"That would be most kind of you."

Baroness Helga and Countess Lilli didn't cast another glance at Mazursky and Dexter, as the ladies led the officers into their home. Mazursky and Dexter were left standing alone on the front porch. They looked at each other, shrugged at the vicissitudes of life, and went off in search of the quartermaster.

As dusk fell, they were sitting around an open campfire, eating beans and Spam with the other GIs. They wore new green fatigues and wore new steel helmets. They shot the shit with the other soldiers, telling all manner of war stories, some of them true, and occasionally they glanced at the living room window of the mansion, from which came the sound of music and laughter. Baroness Helga and Countess Lilli were entertaining the American officers, giving them cigars, dancing with them, and who knew what other favors they would bestow on them.

In the morning, Mazursky and Dexter were driven by jeep to a huge repple-depple (replacement depot) in the rear. It was located on a former German Army post, and they stayed there for a few days awaiting orders, enduring medical examinations, and submitting to the questions of officers from various Intelligence sections. Finally their orders arrived; they were to be returned to their former units.

On the appointed morning they packed their few belongings together and carried them to the motor pool. A transportation officer told them to board trucks parked in front of the motor pool. They were assigned different trucks.

DOOM PLATOON

They stood in front of ten trucks being boarded by soldiers returning to active duty from hospitals, POW camps, and Rest and Recuperation Camps.

Mazursky held out his hand. "Well, so long, buddy," he said to Dexter.

"It's been nice knowing you, Mazursky."

"Good luck, and keep your head down, you scumbag."

"You too, asshole."

They shook hands and slapped each other on the back. Then they picked up their gear and boarded their respective trucks. One by one the trucks pulled away from the motor pool and headed for the front lines.

The End

AFTERWORD

I CONFESS THAT I'M FASCINATED BY WAR, probably because I was raised on it. I was only four years old in Massachusetts when Germany invaded Poland, and six when Japan bombed Pearl Harbor.

As my mind formed, it filled with news of war including regular reports of local men killed and wounded. Often it seemed that the Allies were losing, and America would become occupied by fanatical Nazi murderers and/or diehard Japanese head-choppers.

Not only was World War Two impacting me daily, my father was a World War One veteran, having served with the famed Second Division in six major battle engagements, wounded at Chateau-Thierry. A two-inch diameter sunburst scar was visible near his left temple to his dying day.

We lived together alone, my mother having passed on. Pops managed our apartment like a barracks, he the sergeant and I the private. As I grew older, I read many articles and books about war, trying to make sense of how and why nations went to war, and how and why soldiers could bring themselves to kill total strangers.

I enlisted in the Army in 1954 at age 19, because I wanted the G.I. Bill for college. It was during the Korean War. Peace talks were underway at Panmunjon, so I assumed the war would end officially soon, and I'd enjoy a peaceful military career in some exotic post like Tokyo, wearing my snazzy Ike jacket, surrounded by beautiful women.

Instead, we 'cruits were taught that North Koreans and Chicoms were treacherous, the ceasefire wouldn't last, and we'd better pay attention to instructors because our next assignments probably would be the front line in Korea, with actual bullets whizzing through the air, and real artillery shells bursting nearby.

During training I fired .30 and .50 caliber machine guns, threw live hand grenades, became semi-deafened occasionally by artillery blasts, followed huge, lumbering tanks into mock attacks, and crawled across the muddy infiltration course at night, live machine gun fire overhead. I learned that war was not at all glorious, but dirty, noisy, bloody, brutal and grotesque for frontline soldiers.

Sergeants thoroughly indoctrinated us in the combat mentality. Often I fantasized killing people, or about me getting machine gunned, or blown to smithereens by an artillery shell. Soldiers were trained to follow orders instantly, without thinking. I fell in line like virtually all 'cruits, because hellhole stockades seemed far worse.

After training I was assigned to the 53rd Infantry Regiment in Alaska, becoming a regular soldier carrying an M-1 rifle and then a Browning Automatic Rifle (BAR), which was heavy, cumbersome, and tended to jam. About a year later I was transferred to the 4th Engineers, who were combat engineers, constantly training to build or blow up bridges and other structures in hotspots, and laying and detecting minefields, often at night. The British call such soldiers "sappers."

During my three-year enlistment, I met many veterans of World War Two still on active duty. One of my sergeants had survived the Bataan Death March. After a few beers or during chow while on maneuvers, sometimes the old sergeants told stories. All were very tough guys. Many actually had killed people. I admired them greatly and still do.

After mustering out, I attended Michigan State University on the GI Bill and signed up for many history courses, which meant reading more about war. After graduating in 1961, I continued war research in my spare time.

When I became a novelist, naturally I wanted to write a war novel. When the time came to actually sit down and put words on paper, I decided to set it during the most dramatic battle of the war in the European Theater of Operations. My top two possibilities were the D-Day Normandy landings or the Battle of the Bulge. The latter won out. I saw in my mind's eye a platoon of soldiers caught up in the middle of the German onslaught. Naturally the platoon would be led by a badass sergeant like the badass sergeants I served under. Sergeant Mazursky also was based on a friend of mine named Mike Nichols, who'd been a World War II veteran and was a tough guy and former prison inmate. I often hung out with him in New York City and he influenced me considerably, for better or worse.

DOOM PLATOON was followed by 35 more war novels written over the course of my so-called literary career, which also included crime novels, spy novels, westerns, and every other kind of novel except science fiction, a total of 83 published novels written under 22 pseudonyms.

I never wanted to sanitize or glamorize war, but still believe that unheralded acts of heroism are common at the front, because soldiers tend to look out for each other. They also develop sardonic senses of humor rather than go bonkers.

During wartime, combatants tend to hate each other. For the sake of accuracy, these wrathful attitudes are reproduced faithfully in my war novels, which might jolt sensibilities of gentle souls who believe everyone should love everyone.

While writing all my war novels, I tried to be true to history and fair to all parties, while recognizing that evil actually exists, and history fundamentally is a succession of cruel ironies or black comedies illustrating the laws of karma.

DOOM PLATOON always will occupy a special place in my heart, because it was my first war novel.

— Len Levinson

About the Author

Photo by Ray Block

LEN LEVINSON is the author of 83 novels written under 22 pseudonyms, published originally by Bantam, Dell, Fawcett, Harper, Jove, Charter Diamond, Zebra, Belmont-Tower, and Signet, among others. He has been acclaimed a "Trash Genius" by Paperback Fanatic magazine, and his books have sold an estimated two-and-one-half million copies.

Born 1935 in New Bedford, Massachusetts, he served on active duty in the U.S. Army 1954–1957, graduated from Michigan State University class of 1961, and relocated to New York City where he worked in advertising and public relations for ten years before becoming a full-time writer of novels.

He left NYC in 2003, residing first in Aurora, Illinois, and since 2004 in a small town (population 3,100) in rural northwest Illinois, surrounded by corn and soybean fields, way out on the Great American Prairie.

He has married twice, but presently lives alone with his MacBook Pro and a library of approximately three thousand books, which he studies assiduously in his never-ending effort to understand the meaning of life itself.

He has three novels and one non-fiction book in the pipeline.

Paintings of Len Levinson by Ari Roussimov; all rights reserved.

http://www.roussimoff.com

Made in the USA
Columbia, SC
14 January 2025

51692945R00122